This story is a w
incidents are fict
locations, or events is coincidental.

ISBN: 978-1-989206-55-3
Offstage Offerings Copyright © 2020 UNNERVING
Offstage Offerings Copyright © 2020 PRIYA SRIDHAR

OFFSTAGE
OFFERINGS

PRIYA SRIDHAR

PROLOGUE

The best part about theater tours was that people paid more to trespass. Official tours cost about fifty per person and happened once every six months. Unofficial tours went for eighty per person and seemed to happen every time college students felt brave on their birthdays. The guide had a set of keys, carefully replicated in Metalworking 101. They had been passed down from guide to guide because the locks were never changed in the theater.

Theater dust settled around the tour group, the building crumbly with age. They entered through the backstage doors. New signs hung up—DO NOT ENTER, NEW MANAGEMENT. The guide held the door open, counted heads, and then let it shut. The door took a few moments to close, as if it was hesitating. It squeaked shut.

"People died in this theater," the guide said, clicking on a flashlight strapped to her wrist. "One was Maurice Delphine."

Her badge read CASS, which was obviously not her name because the tour was strictly illegal. She had earrings shaped like mermaid tails and an orange and pink backpack. The group—mostly drunk college students—followed with stumbling and shuffling feet. They sloshed drinks—the cheapest beers from the nearby bar. They had previously wandered around a city block where coffee shops and smoothie stores were replacing century-old apartments painted in faded aqua.

"How did he die?" Someone shouted from the middle.

"I'm getting to that," said Cass, the guide with the fake name. "This theater is a killer. Your heart may decide to give out. A ghost may possess you and cause you to walk off the catwalk. Or you may pick up the wrong sword and stab someone right in the chest."

She gestured with her flashlight to mimic stabbing. Backstage was full of cardboard boxes, more dust, and darkened lights. Cass shone her light above them to illustrate the catwalk.

"The year was eighteen-ninety-nine. Maurice Delphine was an established stage actor, master fencer, and all-around eligible bachelor. He was a tall fellow, with a handlebar mustache and hair shorn like sheep wool. His last play was the Scottish one."

"The what?" another person asked.

"We don't say the name in the theater." Cass lowered her voice. "Instead, we call it the Scottish name."

"You mean *Macbeth*?" A random voice said.

There were mild screams through the group, followed by groans.

"Yes." Cass pressed the flashlight to her nose. "It is thought to be a play of bad luck. Saying it in a theater invites disaster. As our actor did..."

Mumbling came from the stage beyond them. People could see lights flickering on and off. Cass assessed.

"It seems some ghosts are here"," she said, her lips pulling over a wild smile.

"But what about the actor?" someone asked.

No one paid attention to them. The group prowled towards the wings.

A large scroll hovered over the stage, surrounded by statues. On closer examination, one could see that the statues were gargoyles, with crumbling pedestals beneath their carved feet. A woman stood, hand pressed to the scroll. Blood trickled down from her palm, splashing on the floor.

"And I swear to pay your price," she said in a monotone.

"Well, fuck!" the guide said, eyes large. Some of the more cognizant and sober members straightened up.

"Isn't this part of the tour?" asked a small girl in the back, loudly. Her white shirt had beer stains, and she wore running shoes.

"Shh," her partner said. He had curly hair and

wore a black university hoodie.

The gargoyle heads swiveled, making a cracking sound. Their carved eyes were dark grey, tiny ears moving up and down.

"Everyone out!" Cass said. Genuine panic entered her voice, altering the group.

Though the woman didn't seem upset; she waved her hands at the group like they were flies to be swatted. One palm had a diagonal cut from the thumb to the pinkie.

"Use them," she said.

The gargoyle's wings opened, as did their mouths. Their tongues and gums weren't stone, but pulsating red flesh. Fangs glinted under the stage lights, which started to wink on and off.

Cass pushed everyone back, in a futile gesture; perhaps she could sense what was happening. The first gargoyle leaped on her, knocking the whole crowd down; its claws ripped her chest open. Red teeth crunched ribs and closed around a still-beating heart.

Hot blood splattered the people behind her. They screamed and slipped on the bodily fluids, trying to slide away from the stone claws.

Then the panic started; it dawned on one particularly stoned member of the group that they had not paid to die. Some tried to run further backstage. Tinier gargoyles waited in the shadows for them, claws outstretched. They pulled eyes from sockets with moist pops and chewed on them like oysters, as the victims stumbled in a new and painful darkness. They fell over the stage stairs, tumbling to the carpet. Stone figures swoped over them, talons pinning them to the ground. Long tongues licked up any blood or vitreous waters and the group writhed and moaned, avoiding tongues in a state of agonized shock.

Only smoldering footprints and a clip from the guide's backpack remained. The gargoyles had backed into the pitch black wings as a woman in heels picked up the molten plastic. It had clotted brown blood and black spots. A smell of charred metal and blood filled the air.

"First things first," the woman said. "We need to invest in new locks."

"Done," the figures in the mist said.

On the street, someone panted. A small girl and her partner dry-heaved on the sidewalk. Their sneakers were scorched, and they were coated in blood. But they were breathing night air, and had not become hot entrails mixing with theater dust.

ONE

The dripping faucet had woken her up. So while pulling on her clothes, Vivian had texted the landlord about fixing the leak. One arm through a shirt, her phone rang.

"Hello?" she said, walking to the corner by the window where there was the best service.

"Vivian, great to hear you're awake," the landlord said cheerfully. "Need that faucet fixed again?"

She grimaced, of course she was awake, she'd only just texted him. Her apartment was a student off-campus one, where it had promised luxury living. Vivian supposed in hindsight that the *luxury* standard didn't have a high bar to cross. The owner was subletting for the vacation while they went back home to visit relatives. Vivian hadn't been able to stay in the dorms during the summer, and she hadn't wanted to move back home. If she did, her parents would have been hovering and hinting about all the chores she had neglected while living two hours away.

"About the leak," the superintendent said, "I'll get to it when I have the time. Our usual repairman is on vacation."

"Right, thanks," Vivian said. She hung up and sighed. It was 7:00 in the morning and way too early to be awake. She had to be at the theater by 9:00 AM and it would take thirty minutes by train when most people were getting to work and trying to save time. The superintendent was only not busy around this time because the other, real apartment attendees were a higher priority. She would move out by the end of the summer. The DeMarcos, if they raised the complaint, would be a higher threat.

She couldn't worry about it. Her head was spinning with the facts she had learned about the Haunted Basilio Theater. It was in debt to the city and in danger of being closed down. The summer camp was barely keeping it afloat, operating in the off-season for the last five years. Students had to abide by the harsh curriculum, and there were no refunds if they chickened out and quit.

And they did quit, often.

Under her, the camp had swelled in size. She had previously worked at a for-profit university in Texas that was facing lawsuits for defrauding students. So she had experience working with less than optimal surroundings.

Phone buzzing. She checked the message and wrinkled her nose. It was her old boss.

Hey! I can squeeze you in for one shift when the movies are playing on Saturday nights. What do you say?

Vivian considered typing a brief *Nope!* but paused. There was no guarantee that she could survive several hours with a bunch of hellions. Besides, she didn't want to be the clichéd movie star that ended up isolating her friends only to go back to them. Besides, more money always meant more funds for breakfast and replacing filters in the coffeemaker.

I say make sure no one steals my shift.

She made herself coffee—instant—and ate some sugar cubes rather than mixing them. Today's croissant tasted like a folded envelope of butter and dough. She went with it. Maybe with the two hundred dollars for salary, she could afford the fancier stuff from independent bakeries.

Another text. This one was from Eris.

Good luck! Boule gives you a high-five!

A picture of Boule batting the screen with his paw. There were flecks on the image; fish guts she supposed, from dry treats.

Good kitty, Vivian responded. She absentmindedly brushed her pants; spending the night at Eris' place meant shark movies, beer, and clumps of cat hair. Boule was a serial shedder. Even though Vivian hadn't spent last night there, habit ghosts were hard to exorcise.

Her apartment always seemed less glamorous after she came back from a visit with Eris. It wasn't Eris' fault; she had some work as a grad student and musician, so she could afford a nicer place. But still, it made Vivian think she should switch to an obscure, but valuable major such as physics so she could get the constant reimbursement. It would at least help with the bills. A shame that math and science had always eluded Vivian.

—

This morning blazed. Fortunately, the train had the air-conditioning running full blast, freezing anyone dressed in a casual tank or t-shirt.

Vivian had a denim jacket. She swore she saw a girl leaning against a man in a checkered business suit to share their body heat. Eventually, someone on the PA would announce, "Please remember to watch your personal space." Or at least they would once they got to the luxury stops.

The theater was in the middle of Orange Canopy and near Citrus Strolls, because the city had once been a collection of groves that collected oranges and lemons to sell to sailors. It had a large limestone facade, with grimy glass windows that extended from the ceiling or floor.

To get to the theater, she needed to walk five blocks to the left of the train station and go through the chain-link fence. In its heyday, lines stretched away from the facade, down across the street, and vendors would sell ice cream to the people waiting. Theatergoers clicked Jimmy Choo heels onto carpeted floors and smoked cigars behind tinted car windows, leaving wads of cash in donation boxes.

She hunched up, trying not to touch anyone as the train rocked. Now that she had the job, she wasn't sure if this was a good idea. Sometimes she barely had patience with her teenage coworkers at the ice cream stand next to the movie theater. Why would she have patience now? What if she yelled at one for not taking the performance seriously? What if she messed up a kid?

Going to the theater the second time made Vivian feel heavier. She wore a casual button-down shirt and khaki pants. The attire suddenly felt totally wrong for the part. She took out her phone and checked the time.

Screeching and a slowing of gears. The rhythmic forces faded. The train ground itself to a halt.

Vivian looked up from her phone. She had ninety-five percent battery power, which should be enough.

"Please excuse us," an announcer said over the PA in a monotone voice, "we are experiencing some technical difficulties. Stay in your seats and stay in the train until we are moving again."

Vivian tapped her fingers against her phone. This wasn't happening. She was early. Out of the house with a ten-minute window!

Other passengers muttered to each other; one eyed her the way a fish eyed a cricket before swallowing it. Vivian looked through the window. They were on a part of the railing over the nearby park. No chance of running out and hoping she could sprint in time.

This was bad, this was bad. She could not be

late. Her thoughts spun like whirling gears

"They do this every time."

"Summer heat screws with everything."

"I think they're planning to go on strike because of all those tax cuts."

"It's the damned liberals."

"How you figure that?"

The train car doors flew open. Everyone looked up as an alarm beeped.

"Have you all been saved?" a girl asked. She had blond hair

"No, and no thank you," Vivian said. "I'm busted."

They locked eyes. Vivian's phone vibrated in her hand. A name flashed in white letters; the girl saw it. She blinked.

"I know her," she said.

"That's my boss." Vivian's cheeks reddened.

The girl snuffled. Then she lunged forward, grabbing the phone.

"Hey!" Vivian struggled.

"Don't go!" The girl said. "People went bloody! Let me save you!"

"Can you stop trying to save me?" Vivian asked, thrashing. "'That's mine." Vivian grabbed her phone back.

"Hey, stop that!" The businessman said. He pulled the other girl off Vivian

"You'll die!" The girl screeched.

"Bug off," the man said, pointing.

The train doors slammed. It looked like the girl was shuffling from car to car.

"Are you okay?" The businessman asked Vivian.

"Yeah. Fine," she muttered. Her phone was no worse for wear. That was something.

Suddenly, the wheels moved and Vivian snapped out of her violent mood. Everyone gave a collective sigh in relief. Marian had sent a reminder about clocking in on time for orientation. She debated texting Marian to say she'd be late, but there were still four minutes left in the window. Maybe she wouldn't disgrace herself.

Yeah, *maybe*.

—

The train stopped with a deafening screech. Vivian hopped up and practically ran. She wasn't late, but the clock implied that she would be if there wasn't a hustle factor.

Being booted out of the theater on her first day would not be fun at all. Then it would mean begging for more shifts via text messages, and more passive-aggressive texts from her mother.

Nope, she didn't want that. Better to show that she was a real adult. She would not admit that the trains had sabotaged her.

She practically skipped three steps at a time down the escalator from the train to the ground level. If a security cop hadn't been watching with beady eyes, Vivian would have hopped the turnstile—could she do it in cheap twenty-dollar slip-on shoes? In bare feet and yoga pants, she totally could.

Just a few more feet. She hustled past the tobacco shop. Past the chain-link fence, *don't drop your cellphone*.

"There you are," the security guard said.

Vivian panted and stopped. Any relief the train had provided with air-conditioning had vanished. Sweat drenched her from head to toes and was making her hair stand up on end.

"Am I late?" Vivian gasped.

"Nope. Right on time." The guard gestured at the clock right behind her. "Next time don't oversleep or miss your alarm though, young lady."

"Glad you remember me," Vivian panted, thinking it was best not to correct her about what happened. "Can I get past you?"

"Sorry, you need to sign in." The guard handed her the clipboard. "Be sure to print your name. The ink can smudge easily."

The clipboard weighed on her hands. Vivian fumbled with the pen and wrote her name in an illegible scrawl. The pen had leaked. She rubbed at the ink smudging her fingers. The clock ticked. One minute past, making her late by default.

"You'll get a photo ID after this," the guard said. "It will let you go to any part of the theater. Also, it gives you a discount on any performances."

"Useful," Vivian said. A hint of sarcasm buried in her tone. A theater discount wouldn't help her if she was fired.

"Very." The guard nodded, still not moving.

"I thought the theater hadn't hosted performances in a long time." Vivian made a gesture, signaling she still needed to get inside.

"There are a few scheduled this summer." The guard shrugged. "Maybe we got a lucky streak this year. Could also be Marian's fundraising paid off. The woman's a machine."

Maybe. It still seemed weird. A theater that had no recent performances was suddenly open? Not that Vivian was complaining.

"This way." The guard ushered her to the back of the theater, finally, to the same place where she had interviewed. The theater had once been splendid, with plush carpeting and starch white marble tiles. Now the carpet had run down spots in some areas, and the corner tiles had cracks. It reminded Vivian of when cobwebs gathered in the apartment, in the darkest corners. She shuddered through her panting.

She and the guard approached a set of doors disguised to match the walls. The guard opened them to reveal a bland room with fluorescent bulbs that lit the office in a faded yellow, as if it were the afterthought of someone's dandelion field.

"Hey, Marian, here's the last one," the guard said with a big smile.

Marian looked up from her clipboard. She had ringlets of dark brown hair the color of the stained mahogany. Her suit was checkered grey, like the sky when it couldn't decide on bringing the rain down or not.

Twenty counselors sat around rectangular tables. They looked up as Vivian stumbled in. People like her, though varying in accessories. One had pierced rings through his eyebrows, while another had a tattoo of a butterfly on her bare shoulder.

"Hello," Vivian said, catching her breath. "Nice to meet you all."

"Glad you made it." Marian tapped a clipboard. "You all need to fill out your tax information so you can all get paid. Next time ensure that you arrive on the agreed time."

Vivian nodded and sat at the only free chair. Her cheeks went red. She clenched her fists within her jacket.

"Go easy on her," the tallest counselor said. He scratched one eyebrow piercing. "Not everyone can be as perfect as you."

"Yes, Harper." Marian nodded stiffly. "You've made your opinion clear on perfection. Regardless, we must hold up standards."

The counselors watched, as if spectators

witnessing a tennis match.

"Everyone, fill out your paperwork," Miriam said. "Make sure it's neat."

She closed the door behind her as she left. Her heels clicked against the tile floors. Vivian wanted to rest her head on the table and hoped this bad start passed quickly. Papers rustled around her.

"Harper, you really shouldn't tick her off," Drew said. She was the one with the tattoo.

"She shouldn't be roasting someone who probably made it on time. It's one minute."

Vivian closed her eyes. Then she took a deep breath. Paperwork. Get it done. Simple.

Twelve counselors flipped through the pages. They all had Haunted Basilio Theater pens. Vivian reached for one from the center of a cluster. Her form had the edges dog-eared and looked like a coffee mug had sat on the left side. Vivian shook her head and wrote around the brown stains.

"Good morning!" Drew said in a chirpy voice. "Are you new here as well?"

"Very," Vivian said. She chewed her lip when trying to remember her social security. "How about you?"

"It's my second year. I'm Drew."

"Vivian." She filled out her address. Another thing to remember, that it was her temporary sublet for the summer and not her dorm mail. That was one thing to not take for granted, how the mail would just come in to one box and wouldn't need to be picked up from the front desk.

Dates of birth, IDs, surnames, marital status. Many boxes to fill, a signature, and a date to scrawl in a tiny rectangle. All this paperwork was so mundane. On the other hand, it meant that she would get her $250. That would be no small change. Vivian made her fingers loosen around the pen so she didn't clamp on it.

"So, how is the regular camp life?"

"You'll love it," Drew said. "The best part is how the kids always surprise you. They say the funniest things."

"The camp's been around for a while, then?" Vivian asked. "I saw the ads in the newspaper. Someone on campus came to recruit."

"It's on the down-low," the guy with the ear-piercings said. "We were all hired the year before because our colleges did discreet recruiting. I guess we were the beta test to make sure this could work for more parents."

"Huh." Vivian brought her pen to her teeth. She closed her mouth just in time before biting the plastic end. No need to make a bigger fool out of herself.

"Yeah, it's weird." The guy offered his hand. "I'm Harper."

"Yeah, I heard." Vivian winced. Harper had quite a grip, but not bone-crushing. Marian's grip had nearly broken Vivian's fingers.

"So am I the only new person?" she asked.

"Nah. Sergio and Joycie are new," Harper replied. "So are Damon and Sallie. Poor guys; they have the little ones."

He gestured to a group of four at the other end of the table. They all seemed to huddle. Sallie had streaks of blue in her otherwise blond hair. Sergio was the shortest of the group. Joycie had fingerless gloves while Damon scratched a boil on his neck.

"The little ones?" Vivian asked.

"The smaller age groups," Drew supplied. "So kindergarteners up to second grade. They're adorable, but, man, are they energetic. You can't get them to sit still for anything. We have to jump through hoops to get them to pay attention."

"I look forward to it," Vivian said with a sardonic edge. Trying to spoon-feed serious acting lessons was totally not her thing.

"Fortunately, you have the middle group," Harper said. "The second and third graders. So, not so young that they'll tire you and not so old that you'll feel jaded."

"Which group do you have?"

"The teens. They make me feel old and jaded. They assume I'm fifteen. I don't bother correcting them."

"Sounds like you're a pro at this," Vivian said, trying to tone down the sarcasm, she didn't want to sound envious.

"Trust me, you become a pro after spending most of your day with them." Harper placed his pen diagonally on his papers. "Ready to hand these in?"

Vivian filled in the last box on her papers. She gathered them and tried to wipe away the brown stains.

"Here." Drew handed her a paperclip with a bent edge.

"Thanks." Vivian poked a hole, trying to clip the papers. "Oh, shit."

"Don't worry. You'll just have to fill it all out again if it doesn't meet Marian's standards," Harper said cheerfully.

"Haha." Vivian passed it to the pile that was gathering next to the scattered pens. "What do we start with, even?"

"We watch a video on what the camp represents, and Marian will tell us we need to look like real adults and not actors." Harper pointed at his piercings. "Then I argue with her every day this week that it's healthy for kids to see piercings because it exposes them to more in the world. These babies will have to go during the day and I'll put them back in at night."

"Then why wear them on day one?"

"Because it's only orientation," Harper said. "I'm hoping to make Marian change her mind. I'll wear her down one day. I'm fighting for the principle to wear what I want."

"If you weren't so good with kids, she'd dock you for insubordination," Drew said. "I swear she's ready to fire you the minute she finds a docile counselor with no earrings at all."

"The day she fires me is the day the theater is set on fire. She needs me and she *loves* me."

"Ha. I don't know how you do it." Drew's response had envy tinged within it as well, and Vivian felt a little better.

"You aren't patient enough with them. Wait for them to want to nap."

A laugh escaped Vivian's mouth. She tried to cover it with a cough. Harper winked at her.

"You'll get used to it," he said. "Between the kids and the admin, I'd rather fight the admin. Rock against the system!"

—

"Welcome to the Haunted Basilio Theater Camp," a disembodied voice announced. She had a nasal tinge that would hypnotize you to sleep while machines came in the night and chopped you up to put in a can to sell at a grocery store.

"Who knew that VCRs still existed?" Drew whispered.

"Not me," Sallie responded from across the room. "I guess someone in tech and crew here must be a video cassette wizard."

Vivian covered her yawn. This was exactly how

bad movies started with fake dystopias. She hoped that this camp wouldn't turn out to be a Soylent Green factory. But then, being cut up and canned would be a suitable alternative to figuring out where she'd audition after graduation or if she'd need to get a boring office job. She probably shouldn't mention that.

"As a camp counselor, your job is to monitor your kids and give them an appreciation for the theater." Images appeared of other counselors working with toddlers. The toddlers painted trees with markers at odd sizes and proportions.

Sallie doodled during the video on a spare sheet of paper, using a permanent marker. The smell filled the room, making Vivian's head spin. Harper flicked his fingers off his eyebrow piercings. Drew checked messages on her phone discreetly. Her eyes wandered to the shadows behind the TV. A shape high up on the wall skittered, dripping something red. Vivian recoiled as a red drop splashed near her hands. It looked like rusty water. She told herself that.

"Why would anyone want to send their kid to a haunted camp?" she whispered.

"It looks good on their resume for acting gigs and keeps the kids entertained," Harper whispered back.

"We also expect you to contribute to the culture of the program and to set an example for your students." Counselors in blue t-shirts posed in front of admiring kids. "Dress code will teach your students to arrive with neat clothes and hair. Spitting out your gum and chewing with your mouth closed will inspire them to not arrive with chewed gum."

"Robot kids," Drew whispered. "No one ever stands that still, unless they're artificial."

"Or unless they're a model," Harper responded. "Sometimes the kids have to sit real still so that nothing happens."

"Shh!" said one short woman with straight black hair.

"Sorry, Xanthia," Harper said. He and Drew muffled their giggles through open palms. Vivian felt her mouth twitching, though she would not laugh. The video felt like overkill.

"Remember that we are here to educate them and teach them to have fun during the summer," the video went on in that same disembodied voice. "These children will grow up and become performers. They need to learn how to master the stage and how to act with their full heart and soul. The ones that cannot make it should leave with hope in their heart. The ones that can, should become the divas of the future."

Now *that*, Vivian could embrace. She knew that acting wasn't easy. Few had success. But a kid had to learn that early on before adults lied and just cut you, saying nothing. If you taught them the ropes, then they could surprise you. Actors could be remarkable if given the chance. She would help people step in the right direction since no one had taught her when she was a child.

"Now go out there and be the best counselor for the Haunted Basilio Theater."

The video ended, putting the room in semi-gray darkness. All the counselors looked at each other. Xanthia played with her hair.

"So what do we do now?" Vivian whispered.

"Marian's got the video length memorized," Harper said. "In five seconds, she'll come in and start with round two of orientation."

He started counting down with his fingers. Vivian noticed the length of his dirtied nails. She wondered if that was part of his statement and the principle that went with arguing for the right to wear his piercings.

"Okay then." Marian came into the room just as Harper reached his last finger. "I take it you all enjoyed the video."

A chorus of "Sure" followed. Xanthia, the short woman who had shushed Harper and Vivian, gave a shrug. Marian had turned to remove the cassette from the VCR and didn't see it. Her skirt had a loose thread hanging out from the side and Vivian had to fight the urge to reach out and pull it.

"So, we need to talk about our curriculum for

the summer and how we want to improve from last year," Marian said. "The parents were impressed, but not convinced that we had what it takes to revive the theater. Most of the kids also want works they already know, rather than some obscure skits that we can get for free. So, sadly, unless you have fairy tales, none of you can contribute your scripts this year."

"What?" said several other counselors, Xanthia the loudest. A load groan echoed from those who hadn't spoken.

"I know you're disappointed." Marian placed the VHS in a plastic case. "But the kids are our harshest critics. If they say that they don't like your work, then they don't like it. We can't take chances this year. Plus, I catch if one more of them swearing between auditions and callbacks—"

Vivian sat straight and up to attention.

"Kids don't know how to appreciate art!" Harper said.

"Since you didn't submit a script, you have no personal investment in this, Harper," Marian replied dryly. "Please don't cause trouble."

Groans settled around the room. Vivian blinked. The word *curriculum* sounded foreign to her. Did summer camps have lesson plans?

"Counselors always get input," Harper said under his breath, seeing Vivian's confusion. "But I guess they're letting us have less input this year."

"So our goal is to put on one play a month with the kids." Marian handed out packets. "Look through these options. These were the only ones on which we could get licenses. Some are short plays, and others are full shows. With the skits, we may do several at once."

All the counselors flipped through the printouts. Sallie looked bored as she made marks with a pen. Xanthia took colored markers from her jacket pockets.

Vivian didn't even bother to get a writing implement. She skimmed. Each age group had their selection of plays. The little kids had fairy tales—*Cinderella* with a funk twist and a disco-dancing prince, *Three Little Pigs* engaging in a sandcastle contest, or *Snow White and the Seven Lord of the Rings*. That seemed a little reaching. There was one tale she didn't recognize, *The Snow Queen* since it differed from the movie *Frozen*. This one featured a queen kidnapping two children and their attempts to escape her castle. Maybe that would be better for an ambitious end-of-the-summer project. They'd need lots of white paper for snow.

Vivian looked at the options for her age group, which would handle more complicated stuff. A Charlie Brown skit, a sanitized *Saturday Night Live* medley. *The Wizard of Oz*, which was always a class favorite. You couldn't go wrong with any wizards or lions.

"No Scottish play," Harper said.

"Even here, we don't say it?" Vivian asked.

"I'm not going to risk it," Harper said. "It's a theater where the walls are soundproof. You wouldn't hear any of the bad luck or people snapping their neck."

To emphasize, he tightened his hands around his neck and stuck out his tongue. Vivian shivered. Then there was the teens' selection of plays. All with thicker paragraphs and some with bolder fonts and warnings. These selections made her raise her eyebrows: *Grease*, *The Age of Reptiles*—whatever that was; Vivian had never even heard of it—and *The Hunchback of Notre Dame*.

"*Hunchback*?" she muttered. "Are you kidding me?"

A memory of French class, of trying to muddle through the classics that their teacher had mandated they at least try. No kiddie tales of French wine being stomped with grapes in the countryside. It was all depressing Victor Hugo.

"So, any thoughts?" Marian asked.

"*Grease* will be tough," Sallie said. "It has a lot of swearing, drinking, and references to casual sex in it. You'll get angry parents."

"We can edit those out." Marian waved her hand. "We've done it before in previous summer camps."

"It also has a lot of dancing," Harper said. "The

kids have to move for the dance sequences while singing at the same time. Greasers are no joke."

"We got that," Marian said. "We do choreography based on how energetic and willing the kids are. They can dance remarkably if given the right routine. Is it settled? *Grease* is fine?"

No one spoke. Vivian chewed her lip. *Grease* was easier to perform without all the drinking since it was basically a romantic comedy.

"Very well. Shall we move on?"

"You want to do this play with the teens?" Vivian asked with skepticism. "*Hunchback* I mean. The others are fine."

"Kids are tougher than you give them credit for," Marian said. "Also, we have to keep them interested. Otherwise, they won't read the lines."

"This play is kinda racist and violent." Vivian tapped the paper with her fingernail.

"We can edit that," Marian said. "If Disney can do it, so can we. Besides, the parents complained last year about our fare being boring."

"They may have our heads on pikes instead," Vivian replied. "I say we do the time-traveling one, there's nothing problematic there. It will excite them. Who doesn't like dinosaurs?"

"The asteroid didn't like them," Harper replied. He kept his tone solemn.

A beat. Then a smile nearly broke through Marian's stern look. She ducked her head to hide a laugh. That also broke the tension in the room.

"We may not even get to *Hunchback*. I appreciate your concern, Vivian, but these are just goals. We need to see how willing the kids are to act."

Vivian sank back in her chair. Xanthia was drawing on her copy of the sketch packets.

"I'll make sure that she doesn't approve the play," Harper whispered. "Like I said, she *loves* me."

"Thanks, man," Vivian whispered back.

"All right, so who wants to brainstorm acting exercises? Anyone?"

Harper rolled his eyes in Vivian's direction.

"Make sure that the kids don't overact too much this year," Marian said.

"Kids will overact," Harper pointed out. "They're still learning."

"Just the same, they should learn to tone it down before they become entrenched in all their bad habits."

More hours of this, of talking games and activities that would keep the kids enthralled. There would be a few tubs of stage makeup, but washable; children's face paint was encouraged instead. It was cheaper, could wipe off easily, especially since most counselors would have to buy extra supplies from their paycheck.

Say what? Vivian nearly said before Harper nodded at her.

"Hazard of the trade," he whispered. "We're like teachers; sometimes we have to pay for the extra supplies. But we usually have enough."

"Boo," she whispered back.

"And remember, the basement and roof are off-limits for everyone," Marian finished. "Both are still dirty and need renovation."

Vivian lifted her head from a haze of makeup talk and the revelation she'd have to sacrifice some of the money she hadn't even earned. None of this made any sense, except not going to parts of an old theater.

"We're totally going to the basement," Harper whispered. "We'll just need to make sure the kids don't. That'd be a terrible liability."

"Man, you are a troublemaker," she said. "Are you trying to get fired?"

"I'm trying to live. I've already found the way to the roof."

Vivan tried not to smile. More red dripped from the ceiling, but she made an effort to listen to Harper. This was day one on the job.

TWO

In the basement, pipes creaked. They ran parallel to

the walls, within an extra antechamber. Each one leaked red fluid. The cracks betrayed mold and extra stone dust clinging to the inner workings.

Bones littered the floor; most were a few weeks old, some brittle. Statues loomed above them, fabric snarled in their teeth.

—

"He said that?" Eris swigged her beer. "Wow."

"No kidding," Vivian said. "That guy's not afraid of Marian. Or anything, it seems."

They were in Eris' apartment, sprawled on the floor. Eris' hair was wrapped in curlers and she wore a tie-dyed t-shirt that sagged to her knees.

"She sounds like a total bitch."

"It's her job. I'm just relieved she didn't fire me."

"Nah, the trains weren't your fault. It was probably a test to see if you could follow instructions and be a sheep. Well, you are eighty percent a sheep."

"Sheep aren't docile," Vivian replied. "I've seen them on farms at petting zoos and as part of a high-school rotation of Four-H. They bite if they don't like you. Why do you think we have more lamb chops than mutton chops?"

"Because lamp chops are tender?"

"Okay, good point." Vivian sighed. "I'm screwed if this place gives me the boot. I can't get any more parlor shifts."

"It's fine. You can watch my cats."

Vivian snorted. Eris had three inky-black cats, which were normally affectionate, but had decided to be aloof. Boule had curled up under the heat lamp Eris kept for the winter; she had it turned on, despite the heat. He had rested his tail on the switch so that no one could turn it off without getting a dirty look and claws swiped at them. Botard was playing with the fake fish in the fishbowl, splashing her paw in and out. And Baguette was napping on the windowsill, paws twitching in her sleep. She was the oldest, and thus the mellowest of the three.

Vivian leaned back. Eris' apartment was larger than hers. There were throw rugs everywhere and walls that had insulation coming out from certain cracks. She was practically in another city to take advantage of the fantastic rental rates. Though it was only a thirty-minute drive away, and Eris had a car, Vivian marveled at the difference. If she hadn't found the sublet for the summer, she might have begged to stay with Eris as a cat-sitter.

"So you survived day one. You know what that means?"

"That now I have to survive the rest of it?"

"No, it means movie time." Eris reached for the remote. "Are you in the mood for terrible shark films or romantic comedy?"

—

The next few days of orientation flew by fast. Vivian spent them going through trial runs of games, to see if the campers would know the differences between stage right and stage left, and if they could improvise.

She, Harper, and Xanthia sometimes met for dinner after; Harper knew a great Asian fusion place that gave student discounts and large orders. They talked about their plans on how to teach the kids. Then Harper would steal all the egg rolls and give the girls his fortune cookies.

They also explored the theater on their lunch breaks. Harper seemed to know his way around, finding doors that mysteriously opened to his touch. Drew sometimes joined them, but other times she was the lookout. She'd text to alert them whenever they were in danger of Marian finding them. Marian also reminded them of the obvious: no posting forbidden rooms on social media.

One day, Harper took them up a flight of stairs hidden behind one of the balconies. The olive-green steps had cracks and dust, making them all cough and hop over crumbled stairs. There was a strong smell of rotten flowers, mixed with strawberry air freshener.

"So you know the places Marian told us not to go?" Harper asked as he produced a set of keys.

"Dude, you'll get busted," Xanthia said, stumbling to the safety of a doorway.

"They're the spare keys left in storage. No one even notices when they're missing."

"Still," Xanthia frowned, "why do you trust us?"

"Because you're my accomplices." Harper jiggled a silver jagged key into a round doorknob. "Remember, it's going to be the new ones. These locks were just installed."

Vivian bit her lip hard enough to find skin to chew. She could almost hear Miriam's curt dismissal and being forced to turn in their t-shirts. Vivian would miss that ugly-synthetic smell.

A few wiggles and he swung it open. A cloud of dust followed. Harper waved his hands in a dramatic gesture.

"Harper, you are a maniac." Xanthia rubbed her eyes.

"Wow." Vivian breathed a deep, clear breath. "What a great view!"

You could see the ocean from here, and sailboats as part of the yacht club. What's more, the sky had clouds that just touched the horizon.

On the roof, pigeons roosted. Construction equipment, piles of bricks, and cement blocks. The equipment had gathered rust and sunburns. Beyond that, though, they could see the rest of the neighborhood. The bay glittered in the distance.

The pigeons saw them, chittered, and charged. Their wings flapped against the wind.

"Hey!" Harper shielded himself.

"Shoo!" Vivian waved at them.

The birds cawed and flew away. Feathers dropped like dirty snowflakes.

"Okay, that was not what I meant to show you," Harper said.

"Fucking birds," Vivian said, brushing feathers off her hair. "What startled them?"

They walked around the equipment, wondering how all the cement blocks and sandbags fit together to make a new theater roof. A pile of broken glass made it seem like a diamond had shattered. Vivian carefully maneuvered around it. Even with her sneakers, she had a memory of how one time a piece of glass had gotten lodged in her heel and it stuck out like a bad nail. The pain had run up and down her leg with sharp jolts. Once was enough, even with the help of ointment and Band-Aids.

"We could get in so much trouble," Vivian said. "Marian told us specifically *not* to come up here. Or the basement."

"Worth it," Harper said. "If they ask, tell them I blackmailed you because I found a picture of you from a wet t-shirt contest."

"Ha!" She punched him. "As if I would ever do such a thing."

"Same goes for me," Xanthia said. "Just don't post any pictures to Twitter. Plausible deniability."

"And don't trip over any of those cement blocks," Harper said.

Vivian walked to the roof's edge. She could see the movie theater with her ice cream parlor from there. People below milled about the shops and restaurants. It was like seeing everyone as dolls or doll-sized. Vivian felt powerful from the thought.

"This is so cool," she said. "Cooler than that hidden costume room. Though that's still awesome."

"Want to stop by there on the way back?" Harper asked.

—

The hidden costume room was behind a wing meant for hosting wealthy guests. Dusty, moth-eaten suits with ruffle collars

"See anything you like?" Xanthia asked. She fingered a soldier's coat meant for an American Revolution reenactment. It had some buttons missing, but a seamstress in the wardrobe department could fix it in a few minutes flat.

"This one." Vivian pulled out a red dress embroidered with a thick golden thread. It had petticoats and a train in the back. Vivian's mother had an anklet that would blend perfectly with the thread. Not that Vivian had the courage to ask.

"That would be perfect for a dancer role." Xanthia slipped her sleeves into the coat. They bunched in at her wrist too tightly.

"Yeah." Vivian fingered the red velvet. It was the exact thing a teenager would wear to dance in the streets, to earn coins from passersby.

She unzipped it. Dust came off from the metal teeth. She put a hand through one of the sleeves. The velvet rubbed against her, and made her think of horses. To put it on properly, however, she'd have to strip completely.

Vivian replaced the dress on the rack. The fabric had faded with time, anyway, and would probably need a thorough cleaning. Discolored red and white alternated in spots. They would need one heck of a tailor to replace that fabric.

The wind whistled around them

"Do you sometimes feel like the ghosts of past performers hang around here?" she asked.

"It is a haunted theater," Xanthia said. "Maybe the ghosts like to dress themselves up in the costumes like Harper said."

"Good point. Who died here?"

She turned with the wind, inhaling the dust and mold that it carried. Fabric rustled around her with soft crinkles.

"A few people broke their necks when falling from balconies," Xanthia said. "Usually that was due to poor construction. But there were weird disappearances, too. Like about ten years ago *Annie* was going on, and you need multiple girl actresses for the lead."

Memories came back. Her parents coming to the city, treating her to a show. Getting dressed in cotton and choosing red tights.

"Right." Vivian took a deep breath. "What about it? What happened to them?"

"Well, after, those girls vanished. From a hit show like that, you'd think they would all become artists. But no. Just went away from the newspapers. Like the show had never been there. Or that people no longer cared."

The show had been fun, actually. Vivian had sat, enthralled, and not said a peep. A curly-haired soprano two years older than her had belted out enough of *Annie* to win Vivian's heart. She had worked with a toy dog that she wheeled along on a makeshift wagon. The dog had been plastered with wool that peeled at the edges.

"That's boring," she said. "Loads of people do that."

"I didn't mean they just went back to their lives. Like, literally vanished. I thought it was a normal washed out child actor tale until the newspapers said they all ran away."

Vivian turned to look at Xanthia. The wind grew stronger, as if to support the story.

"What?"

"Apparently all the girls ran away at once. They left a note, talking about how they were going to sleep over at the theater since they were spending nights there anyway. But the custodians unlocked the doors, and people crawled all over the hidden rooms. If those girls did sleep over here, there was no trace of them. No popcorn bags or pillows, nothing."

Vivian shivered. The room shivered with her. That girl who had been singing on stage, just gone. Like the last notes of a song before the orchestra cut the melody.

"That's so creepy," she said.

"Even creepier, the theater never mentioned it again. But after that, no more plays with kids. Like it's a curse. Maybe all the wind is those girls, if they vanished into the air conditioning. Part of the illegal tours would be trying to find them, and other child actors that just went away."

Vivian tucked her arms into herself.

"Maybe it's the air conditioning," she said. "Can we go now? This story is spooking me."

Vivian wondered if a song could be compressed into an artificial breeze, and ghosts would hang out in outdated ventilation systems, singing along, carrying the tune. Maybe the notes would ring sour when clogged with the dust.

THREE

"There you are!" The ice cream parlor's manager tossed an apron at Vivian. "Nice to see a familiar face."

She hid her scowl under the apron as she pulled it over her head. If the boss had wanted her full-time, he wouldn't have replaced her with teens.

"What's the most popular flavor tonight?" she asked.

"Chocolate chip. Watch that scooper. The handle is getting ice around it and takes ages to clean."

Vivian nodded. She practiced plastering a smile on her face that would show she wasn't staying up for eight hours to accommodate her classmates and drunkards there for midnight screenings. Her lips were dry; she needed ChapStick or her smile would ache all evening.

"There we go." Her boss patted her on the back. "Keep that attitude up and maybe in a few years you'll take my place."

The first few customers were kids from a birthday party and a mom and son going to see the newest King Arthur movie. Birthday kids never tipped, and they always wanted whipped cream. Vivian served them chocolate or vanilla swirls and with marshmallows toppings. No one wanted the cherry gelato; they would probably cancel that flavor and a few sad tubs would have to be smuggled home. Vivian didn't love cherry gelato, but it was apt to be free.

"So how is the regular job hunt going?" her boss

asked her during a lull as several kids' movies played at once.

"It's going," she said noncommittally while checking the tubs of vanilla—their classic standby. No need to mention that she was committing adultery via a normal day job. "I'm surprised you wanted me back, man."

"Don't sell yourself short. You know other high school students have a curfew?"

"I do." She grinned and pulled on a pair of plastic gloves that made a funny schlepping sound as she squeezed the air out of three of the fingers.

She did the same with the other glove. "Will you open up another parlor by the theater? The Basilio, I mean."

"Why would I? The rent's terrible, and the missus would hate me for life."

"They're opening up again," she said. "You know vendors would go out and sell ice-cream to the people waiting in line?"

"I wouldn't dare," he said. "That place hasn't had a show running in years."

"What?"

"You heard me. The doors are firmly shut. If there were any shows going on, you'd hear it all the way from here. It's not like that theater is soundproof. But it's been quiet, day and night. I know because I'm here every night."

"Hmm." Vivian ran her gloved finger around

the tub lid, collecting icicles. "Good point."

"So it's a nice idea, but it makes little sense." He shook his head. "But we may try selling when the ball games at the park start again."

Vivian wiped her fingers on a napkin, considering what the boss just said.

———

The best part about the second round of day one was that Vivian didn't have to rely on the trains. Sallie had organized a carpool for all the counselors who lived nearby. It meant getting up at 7:00 AM, but it beat public transit.

As soon as Vivian had swallowed her coffee and changed into her standard Haunted Basilio camp T-shirt, her phone buzzed. Sallie was idling outside. A few steps downstairs, with no purse and a pair of jeans.

"Hop in." Sallie drove a maroon family van that had seen better days. One of the back bumpers had fallen off, and someone had sprayed a yellow bat on the side.

"Don't kidnap us," Vivian joked as she clambered into the backseat. She bumped her head on the ceiling. "Ow."

"Careful," Xanthia said. "That also got me."

Vivian rubbed her head and went for the free middle spot. The seatbelt frayed in the center and its buckle was rusty. Definitely, had seen better days.

She didn't buckle up. Harper had his car, so he wasn't there, but Selwyn, one of the newer counselors, was touching up her lip-gloss while sitting next to Vivian. Xanthia sat in the back-back, reading a message on her phone dutifully.

"Looks like most of the kids have their paperwork turned in," Xanthia said. "I hope they like what we're doing."

"I hope they don't wander off," Vivian said. "Or they don't repeat the things that their parents said. Also, I hope they don't get hurt on our watch."

"They won't," Xanthia said. "Kids' bones are like rubber. You know how many times I took a spill while running and always had scabby knees? Happened all the time."

"It's the lawsuits that worry me," Vivian said, also taking out her phone.

Movie on Friday? Eris had texted.

Totally, Vivian texted back. *More bad sharks! Maybe bad sharks falling in love and eating people.*

You know sometimes the babies eat each other?

That's so evil. It could be a movie.

Seeing the city from a car view felt luxurious. Vivian could feel the weight lifting from her shoes. All she had to do was lean back.

Sallie pulled into the parking lot and found a spot. She reached into her shirt pocket for cash. Then she paid the security guard who came to the window.

"We should get a parking permit," Sallie said. "Seriously, we are working here."

"Take it up with the boss," the guard said.

Sallie shook her head as the guard walked away.

"We know that Marian will never agree to that." She opened the van doors. "Come on, let's not be late."

It felt better to come to the theater in uniform, and that the uniform included jeans and sneakers. They would need to move around a lot, on and off the stage, and to ensure that the kids wouldn't be able to outrun them if they got it in their heads to go crazy.

"Are you ready to join the races?" Sallie asked them all. "There's no turning back from all of this."

"No," Vivian replied. "But I don't think I'll ever be ready."

"That's the spirit!" Drew came by and clapped Vivian on the back. "Now, come on. Marian wants to give us one last pep talk in the backroom before we meet the kids."

"More like a death talk," Sallie muttered. "She's got that look..."

"Right, right," Vivian said. All the way to the back, and to where other counselors gathered. They all looked like cotton bluebirds in their t-shirts, checking messages on their phones or bouncing on their feet.

"Where's Harper?" Vivian looked around. No

sign of him, with or without eyebrow piercings.

"Beats me," Selwyn whispered.

"Maybe he slept in?" Xanthia whispered.

"Or he got caught." Vivian's voice quavered at the thought. Maybe there was a rat in their group, or maybe Harper hadn't been careful when returning the spare keys. All it would take was a moment of bad luck or carelessness.

"Doubtful," Drew said. "We'd all be fired. The lady likes to make examples."

"He's probably taking out a piercing," Xanthia said.

Marian walked in, wearing a dark navy suit. She looked very stern and out of place, like a cardinal overseeing robber jays. Vivian shifted from one foot to the other.

"Good morning, everyone," she said. "I trust you are ready. Orientation is first, and then we all get sorted into our age groups. I need you to represent the theater and set an example for your charges. Before that, we have to address some changes."

She took out a sheet of paper and studied it. Her grip was so tight, the paper crinkled. Vivian felt the morning croissant sink to the bottom of her stomach.

"Our lunch area is not adequate to host the kids since the construction company delayed the renovations. We must take the children to the mall's food court, where they can either eat a packed lunch or purchase something."

Okay, that wasn't so bad. It'd be a trek, and they would have to pass the tobacco emporium, but that wasn't *terrible.*

"Second, it seems some counselors have decided to no show. We need to have some of you doubling up to volunteer for their groups."

"Wait, what?" Drew murmured.

"Vivian, you have the eight-to-ten year-olds?" Marian looked her straight in the eye.

"Me?" Vivian squeaked. "I mean, yes, yes I do."

Sweat poured through her shirt. Blushing, realizing that she wanted Harper there, to tell her that Marian was just trying to scare them and was venting her stress out on the counselors who couldn't fight back.

"You and Drew will combine them with the teens. It's not ideal, but with luck, the mix will mean that they all behave."

"Okay," Vivian said. "Sure, fine."

Drew was frowning. She let her sneakers sink into the cracked tiles.

"Harper's in charge of the teens," she said. "Those are his kids."

"Is he sick?" Vivian said.

"Bet he was fired." Xanthia whispered. "So, managing about twice the number of kids? Better you than me. I'd probably kick them to the curb the minute they give me attitude."

She was trying to do the Harper thing, to ease them and make them laugh. Vivian couldn't even bring herself to smile.

"Don't say that in front of Marian," Drew said. She wasn't smiling.

"Maybe they found out about the keys," Vivian said again. "Does anyone have his phone number?"

"I'm on it." Drew started texting. "I'm surprised he didn't tell me. We're tight."

"See?" Vivian threw up her hands. "I'm telling you, this is all weird."

As if agreeing with her, a breeze started up, flowing from the wings of the stage, rustling the curtains. It smelled older than the AC air and practically zapped them with mothball scents. What's more, a putrid scent followed.

"Eeugh! What's that?" Xanthia coughed. "Smells like something died."

"Must be rats." Drew covered her mouth and nose. "Swore I saw one scurrying backstage. I hate rats."

Vivian also covered her mouth and nose.

"Someone needs to tell Marian," she garbled.

"Not it," Xanthia said.

"Nor me or you," Drew said.

As quickly as the hot scent appeared, it vanished.

"Okay, that was weird." Vivian inhaled and

welcomed the theater dust into her lungs.

"Maybe the ghosts know what happened," Xanthia said. "We should ask them."

"You can," Vivian said, shivering. "I'm not paid to talk to ghosts."

—

In the basement, no rats or ants bothered the gargoyles. The rats had gotten wind of stone claws reaching for them, and visited less often. Their squeaks and chitters marked the sound of betrayal, of learning.

Once, a bird had flown in, having navigated from the open backstage door all the way into the dark; a gargoyle had reached forward and bitten off its head, mid-air. The body crashed to the ground, twitching among grey and black feathers. After that, the backstage door was always locked. Now only unsuspecting humans came in, to meet the hungry stone.

FOUR

Orientation happened at several foldable tables, where the parents signed in their kids and ensured that they were going to the right sections.

Vivian helped with handing out name cards and

making sure they were all in order. There were about fifteen kids so far.

Harper should be there, dealing with the kids and their acne and the painfulness of breasts and puberty. But Harper wasn't here. Drew was and Vivian were.

"All right," Drew said. "How about we divide and conquer? You meet with the younger kids, since they're less likely to bite you. Or more likely, depending. You have your rabies shot, right?"

Vivian wrinkled her nose behind the clipboard. She felt her muscles tie into knots.

"I'm joking!" Drew nudged her over. "Trust me, they won't bite. They aren't piranhas."

But then piranhas tended not to bite people. They preferred dead things that didn't move in the water. Vivian felt alive, and she didn't like that. Kids also had an advantage over the fish; they could talk.

There were five or six kids in the younger group. Vivian checked their nametags to make sure she mispronounced nothing and earned Marian's ire. There were two boys and three girls: Derrick, Tara, Cosmo—she read that name twice to make sure it was real and not a prank—Dina, and Marceline. Okay, she could do this.

Derrick was a short kid, with bristly hair. Tara had a curtain of bangs through which she peered with curiosity. Her backpack had her name embroidered, probably by a machine. Dina was the tallest, a skinny girl with unicorn stud earrings and a matching necklace. She also had rhinestones on her nails. Cosmo was the second smallest, with large wooden glasses that looked like they stepped out of a time machine. His hair was wild and unkempt, and he had what appeared to be a comb stuck behind one of his ears. Vivian looked him once over to ensure it wasn't just a trick of the light. He had a book in his oversized jeans jacket. Then there was Marceline, who was the shortest of the lot. She was definitely no older than eight, and her braids reached down to her waist. One of her teeth was loose, and she wiggled it with her tongue.

"Hello there," Vivian said to them. "I guess I'll be working with you."

Tara gave her a look that reminded her of Botard, glaring when Eris wouldn't share chips with him. Vivian's smile faded.

"You're teaching us about acting?" Derrick asked.

"I guess I am. It's nice to meet you all. My name is Vivian." She touched her temporary nametag.

"How much do you know?" Tara fiddled with a thread in her backpack. "And where can I put this down?"

"There's a locker area for all of your things—"

"I want to be the best singer," Cosmo said. His ears pushed his hair out horizontally.

"Are we going to do any dancing?" Derrick asked.

"I want to be like the people in the movies!"

"Will our parents come to see us?"

Vivian waved her hands. The kids did not silence on cue, but they quieted a little.

"One at a time," she said. "I appreciate your enthusiasm."

Drew was right; they were piranhas. The kids were barely holding back from their questions. She answered them to the best of her ability until her voice got ragged.

Marceline was the exception. She watched everyone's waving hands and lodged hers in her pockets. She bounced from one Mary Jane to the other, fidgeting.

A part of Vivian wanted to leave well alone. If someone wanted to be introverted, then it was none of her business.

Drew caught her eye. She gave a disapproving look. Vivian sighed and went over.

"So Marceline, are you excited to be part of the camp?"

Marceline blinked. She wiggled her tooth and nodded.

"I take it you're a young lady of few words," Vivian said. "Don't worry. I know the first day of camp can be overwhelming."

She was lying through her teeth. In all honesty,

Vivian had no sympathy. If you were at camp to act, you had to grit and bear it.

After the question period ended, the teens and kids merged. It was like seeing a time lapse of puberty before her eyes. At least the teens were not the hooligan type, smelling of cigarette smoke or wheeling away on their shoes. Vivian had memories of her high school classmates using wheelies on narrow staircases. They would clatter down, to crash on their knees on concrete floors. There were a lot of visits to the school nurse that year.

"Don't worry." Drew came over. "You won't be alone with the teens. We'll be doing this together."

"Should we switch off?" Vivian asked. "Do you want to get to know the little ones?"

"I have to," Drew said with some philosophy. "Whether I want to, I definitely have to make their acquaintance and go all Mr. Higgins to civilize them. It's not like anyone else can."

There was no arguing that. Vivian sighed and gave a tight nod.

"How are they?"

"Okay, but watch out for Terrence," Drew warned. "He's a spoiled brat, and it kinda shows. But keep your opinion on the down-low, don't want to anger his parents."

Vivian went to the other side to talk to the teens. She plastered on a fake smile. There were only two girls and four boys. One girl had long blond hair with pink streaks that made her look like a heyday Gwen Stefani. Another had dark plaits rolled up into buns like she was Princess Leia.

The boys were different. They were taller for one, slouching. Vivian felt prickles of foreboding. Terrence was the one who had gotten a note; the blond girl was Adaline, while the other was named Maia. The other two boys were Brendan and Kyree. Marian hadn't delivered notes for their profiles; Brendan looked like he could audition for the part of a skeleton with his frame, while Kyree wore a top hat and sunglasses.

"Hello there," she said. "Which one of you is Terrence?"

"I am," the tallest kid said. He was wearing a varsity soccer jersey from his middle school.

"Nice to meet you." Vivian remembered a note about this one. Teachers had kicked him out of school for brawling. Anger issues.

"I'm only here because my parents made me come," Terrence said. He had a buzz cut and some stubble along his chin. Too small to need shaving, but just enough to betray the reasons for his attitude. He clenched his fists.

"We all have parents like that," she agreed. "If you don't want to act, we have other activities in mind."

"I don't dance or paint stupid backdrops."

Vivian clenched her jaw but kept smiling. She

remembered being this shitty as a child to her parents. Seeing it from the other side felt like karmic payback.

"There's also tech, which means handling the special effects," she said. "Some plays even require a cannon or having people float."

"A cannon?" His ears seemed to perk.

"Yeah. Like if you're doing a war story or Tchaikovsky. We can see if we can rig something up here. Or you can choreograph, which means planning what everyone *else* dances. Varsity soccer means you must have some footwork."

That remark broke through his scowl. Terrence nearly smiled.

"I know a few basics of tech and choreography," Vivian offered. "We can get started on that, if it interests you."

"It might." Terrence resumed scowling again.

—

"Okay, I'm bushed." Vivian leaned back on Eris' couch. "And I have to be up for the night shift scooping ice-cream. What a day."

"Oh, come on," Eris said. "It couldn't have been that bad."

"It was." She closed her eyes. "Terrence is such a pill, Adaline is spoiled rotten and cried when Marian told her she couldn't have makeup, and Marceline is just so quiet! It's eerie. Then they all ran off to the food court. Terrence nearly went into the tobacco store and Drew and I had to drag him out, and he threatened his parents would sue us on the grounds of assault. It doesn't help that Terrence is nearly my height, and just as strong."

"Not like he'd beat you up," Eris said.

"Harper would have dealt with him better. I wish he was here with the teens, to reassure me and keep them in line. They were *his* job. He was going to keep us all calm, and he's just vanished."

Harper hadn't answered Drew's texts, and he hadn't shown up at their usual restaurant meet to get takeout.

"Maybe he's too upset to talk to us," Drew had said. "It can't be easy thinking that you are irreplaceable and suddenly you lose your job."

"Give him a few days," Xanthia had said. "I wish I knew where his apartment was. Then we could go cheer him up."

Even with that logical approach to emotions, Vivian had a bad feeling. Harper wasn't the type who would hide away to sulk and not tell anyone about it. He was open about how he felt, at least he seemed like that. She thought she knew people well enough from going to college.

"I think it's just the shock of having a job," Eris said. "Everyone has surprises they'd rather not deal with, but we have to always deal. I ever tell you about the gig where we went to the island and our bus driver got lost?"

"No."

"It was awful. This was before GPSs on phones were a thing. So, you all had to work with a map or a Garmin. We had to navigate because the driver thought a shortcut would be a better idea. A bartender at this Peach Tree Inn had to tell us how to get back on the highway, and we got fined for a toll. The gig's fee barely covered it."

"How was the performance though?"

"It was okay. Made all the people in that church happy."

"That's good."

Eris put on a shark movie—sharks learn how to walk on land and start stalking people through the prairies in the middle of winter. They chatted and drank beer, as the premise wasn't exactly highbrow. It helped that the humans were constantly covered in pink guts.

While a collective CGI mess of carnage flashed the screen, Vivian's mind drifted back to her interview, and the first time she had gone to the theater:

"Pleasure to meet you." Vivian offered her hand. All the career center etiquette dinners talked about the importance of a firm handshake.

Marian's grip was tight; Vivian had to hide a wince. It was like shaking hands with a football player.

"Likewise," Marian said. "Please follow me."

The strange wind seemed to follow Vivian. At the

time, she assumed it was heavy-duty air conditioning. Marian led her through a set of theater doors. They went past the glitzy stage that had once entranced thousands, and went into a series of back doors. Marian opened them to reveal a standard office with fluorescent bulbs that lit the office in a faded yellow as if it were the afterthought of someone's dandelion field.

"So, tell me a little about yourself," Marian said.

Vivian opened her mouth and words spilled. She blathered, unable to keep track of what she was saying, other than, "I am working to get my bachelor's degree in Performing Arts and then getting a doctorate in theater," while also mentioning her haphazard work experience.

In the middle of it, she stopped to take a breath. Marian took that opportunity to ask, "Did you bring a resume? "

Vivian reached into her purse. She pulled out her crinkled sheet of paper and passed it over. Marian's eyes twitched. She took the resume and straightened it. The crinkling echoed between them.

"Hmm." Marian reached behind her and pulled out a manila folder. She took a paper out of it—a printout of Vivian's resume—and compared it to the folded copy.

A part of Vivian wanted to scream, "Why did you need my resume if you had the electronic copy?" The sensible part placed her purse on her lap, where she could clutch it and fidget discreetly.

"Why do you want to be a counselor here at the Haunted Basilio Theater Camp?"

"I really love the theater," Vivian said. "Both as a performance major and as someone who has attended. It would be a lot of fun for me to share it with other kids."

Ninety seconds felt like an eternity, the time you spend gasping underwater as someone holds you down. Or it was the time spent on breathing exercises in Co-op Choir as you made a sizzling sound and massaged your choir mate to warm up for rehearsal.

"It says here that you have internship experience," Marian said. "Do you want to tell me about working on this startup, Friends for Coffee?"

"It was a company that was selling flavored coffee on the go. They needed ambassadors that had charisma. I had a lot of charisma and helped sell it on my campus during special events."

"You only worked there for several months. Why?"

"Oh, the internship had ended. Students couldn't be hired twice."

No need for Vivian to disclose that a huge vat of the coffee had spilled on her during a sales pitch, and the company reps hadn't even noticed when a whole crowd came and wiped her down.

"But I have other activities and experience. You can ask any of my teachers. I'm a hard worker."

"Your resume doesn't list any internships or positions that involve working with children."

"Well, I'm very patient." Vivian managed a tight smile. "I've volunteered in daycares."

"Why is that not on your resume?"

"I ran out of space, ma'am."

They locked eyes for a few moments. Even though Marian looked stern, Vivian relaxed her hands.

"I appreciate you not wasting my time," Marian said.

Vivian considered. She actually hadn't interviewed well, not well enough for her liking at least. Maybe Marian *had* wanted a sheep. Vivian winced, and not because a shark onscreen had just bitten off someone's head.

FIVE

Days blended like pastels in a nighttime art class. Vivian found her energy flagging as she developed instincts to catch kids from running off, both during the day and when they took lunch break. She came to dislike the cheery food court's golden letters spelling out the mall's founder, and how many cars could get discounts on the valet. Most visitors didn't even drive with how scarce parking was, typically.

Terrence was by far the wildest, and Derrick loved the big guy. They would often ask if they could go to the roof and Vivian suppressed the urge to pull a Harper and find the spare key. Drew had given her Harper's phone number, and she kept texting. No response.

Sometimes, when things became too much, she snuck to the stairway leading to the locked basement for a moment of quiet. She thought about Miriam's complete lack of explanation, and how they'd all accepted it. Where was he?

She imagined Harper tying himself to a sailboat, and letting it pull him along the surf. His fingers would hold to the rope, but they would bleed. Perhaps little droplets in the water would bring sharks, hundreds of them into the bay...

A sound pulled her from the reverie.

It had come from behind the locked basement door. She took a step down, whispering, "Who's there?"

"There you are," Drew said, wiping damp hands with a paper towel.

"Okay, any news about what happened to Harper?" Vivian asked when Drew came into the theater from her bathroom break. Drew looked harried.

"No." Drew shook her head. "But Terrence went to the restroom about ten minutes ago. I think he was crying. When I went to check on him, he told me to go away."

"I'll talk to him," Vivian said, stepping away

from the shadowy stairway.

She slipped outside the auditorium doors. Around her, the decaying decadence of a previous era lingered. She swore that she could still smell rotten women's perfume.

Terrence had left the bathroom and was by one of the camp tables where there were free snacks: crackers, gummies, dried apple slices. No one ever touched the apples.

She waited for Terrence to get a snack for himself from the bowl of crackers. Then she walked over. Her sneakers sunk into the carpet.

"Hey," she said.

"Hey. Did Drew send you after me?"

"No. I sent myself to get myself some apples." She toned down her sarcasm.

"Be my guest." Terrence backed away from the table. Vivian didn't come closer.

"You okay, man?" she said. "I'm not a fan of that musical myself."

"It's boring," Terrence said bluntly. He opened the cracker bag and let crumbs spill on the floor.

"Terrence, why were you sent to camp?" Vivian asked. "You seem to be enjoying yourself now. But you said that your parents made you come."

He bounced back from one foot to the other.

"None of your business."

"Of course it's my business," Vivian added. "I really just want to make sure you're okay."

"You're worried about being fired. You know we can hear you."

Vivian sighed. She took a bag of the dried apple slices.

"If you must know, my dad cheated on my mom," Terrence said, "and we found out over Christmas."

Oh. *Oh.*

Vivian replaced the apple slices in the bowl. Even if she liked dried fruit, this was not a time to snack.

"That's awful. I'm so sorry."

"Eh, don't be sorry for me. But my mom? I don't know why she's staying with him." Terrence crammed four crackers in his mouth. "This guy drives around with his younger girlfriend—who is my sister's age—and acts like we can all go on as normal. I say screw him. Awful sonofabitch."

Vivian nodded. She didn't know what to say

"Aren't you going to tell me not to curse?"

"I think you earned that one," Vivian said slowly. "Just try not to say it in front of the other kids. Don't swear in front of Marian, or I *will* be fired."

He managed a grin, but his eyes were sad.

"You know Derrick's mom was going to run the camp. She's friends with my mom. It was her idea to do it and restore the theater. But Marian came through and fought for it."

"Well that's a shame," Vivian said. "I wonder what that might have been like."

"Eh, Derrick's mom is going to try again. She's not someone who gives up."

She had a feeling this would be a more stressful endeavor if she had to deal with a mom as her boss.

"Now, how about we go back in?" she asked. "We're going to do tech in the afternoon. I can show you how to do the flashing disco lights for the kiddie play."

"Okay." Terrence shrugged. "It's a really stupid play."

"Hey, I didn't write the script. I just follow it."

That coaxed a laugh out of him. He tossed his cracker bag into the grey bin next to the table and strolled ahead. Vivian overlooked the table. She froze.

Marian was glaring at them. Perhaps it was seeing a camper where they weren't supposed to be. Or maybe Marian had heard of Terrence's reputation. Surely she couldn't have heard what Terrence said, that another woman was after her position.

Vivian gave her a shrug as if to say, *Hey. I'm doing my job.*

Marian kept frowning. Then she walked into one of the offices. Vivian released her breath in a relieved sigh. She went to the stage doors where Eliza was singing about chocolates, and slipped inside after Terrence.

—

The more humans came, the more they shrunk. This one was the shortest of the lot, scowling like one of the stone brethren. He slid through the doors, which had opened at his touch. Doors obeyed the gargoyles. The last human had keys and was too poky to nibble.

A click, and a light switch. The little one stared. They stared back, stone eyes and open maws. He didn't move as one gargoyle drew a circle. Pink bloomed beneath them. Then it spread all over the room, twinkling under the lights. He screamed as it swallowed him.

They resumed their places. He was too small to eat now. They would let him grow.

SIX

"Is Terrence sick?" Vivian asked the kids as she took roll call.

"He's probably playing hokily," Adaline said with a snort.

"Hokily?" Vivian looked up from her clipboard. "What's that?"

"Some game."

"*Hooky*," Derrick corrected Adaline with a frown. "Where did you hear it was 'hoky-something?' What did you even say?"

"I hope he's not skipping. Hope he's not wandering either." Vivian whirled around. "The roof and basement are off-limits."

"Easy there, Viv." Drew walked in. "Marian told me he's dropping out. Terrence apparently got into trouble at home, so they're giving him a punishment."

That froze Viv. She stared at Drew, who took the roll call clipboard from her.

"What?" she said.

"Terrence got in trouble?" Derrick asked.

"What did he do?" Adaline asked.

"His parents are mad at him," Drew said casually. "So, they said apparently that he couldn't come anymore."

"That doesn't make sense. He didn't want to be here," Vivian said.

"But he's been doing better," Drew replied. "I got him interested in learning how to sift dry ice and all. And he lit up when we found a cannon for him."

She gave a darting look. The kids were listening with interest. Vivian sighed.

"It's a shame," she said. "I really enjoyed having him." To her surprise, she wasn't exaggerating this.

"All right," Vivian said. "We'll draw backdrops

today. Go on, grab the art supplies."

The kids shuffled. Derrick whispered to Marceline, who nodded but didn't smile. Tara fiddled with her backpack, which she refused to leave in her locker space.

"Vivian? A word?"

Vivian turned. Marian popped her head into the doorway.

"Um," she said.

"Go," Drew said. "I'll be fine."

Vivian went, her stomach sinking.

"Am I in trouble?"

"No. But I wanted to give you a heads-up about a change to the curriculum."

Ho boy.

"I know that you were having trouble with our selection of plays," Marian said. "Because of your concerns about the topic material."

"Yes."

"I've found that my choices may interest the kids more than you think, given that you've already lost one of your members." Marian's eyes were hard quartz crystals. "I hoped that you could reform the wilder ones."

Vivian's mouth clammed. Her mind went blank. Terrence not being here wasn't her fault!

"You will help put on *Hunchback*," Marian said. "That is final."

She walked away. Vivian stood there, numb.

Marian's heels echoed through the partly renovated theater, making Vivian think of bones banging against crypt doors, banging and begging for someone to open up.

———

The morning started with a haze. Vivian was flagging. She tried to smile. The grimace ached her chapped lips. Thing was that no balm or ointment could seal the cracks in her temper, which were threatening to leak.

As the young kids sketched out their ideas onto computer paper, some were even making origami out of construction paper, the teens were mixing tempera paints on plastic plates that served as palettes. They wore aprons that Xanthia had purchased and were practicing on a giant roll of paper.

"I can't believe it," Vivian said, stabbing her brush into a tub of paint. Yellow splattered her apron.

"Don't take it personally," Drew said. "She's just doing what's best for the kids."

"Racist plays aren't best for the kids; the *Hunchback* features miscarriage of justice," Vivian replied. "Also, that's not it. It's that we have another play that makes more sense. It would be more fun for them, and we could simplify the effects."

Drew shrugged. "It's not worth losing your job

over a principle. You saw what happened with Harper. All the movies that teach you to stick to your guns are lying because the actors get paid more than we ever will in our lives."

Vivian growled and painted a yellow sun on paper, and then added angry black eyes.

Derrick watched them. He was using Sharpies to draw, despite that it bled through the paper into the table and made the whole room smell like ink.

Vivian squinted at him. She had gotten used to saying this once or twice a day when they talked about scenery and backdrops.

"Wipe that up, Derrick. Can you use something lighter?"

He sheepishly reached for a pencil. Drew opened the door to let the Sharpie fumes escape into the hall.

"Sorry, ma'am," he said.

"You're all doing great," Vivian said. She felt like she was on autopilot.

"I want to do this for the backdrop." Marceline picked up her drawing. "For Paris, you know. With all the hangings, we should make it look nice."

Marceline traced the crayon drawing she made of brick buildings and a long blue rectangle for the river. All her lines slanted, because she was a leftie.

"You want to do a play with hanging?" Vivian asked. "And death and all of that?"

"It's cool," Marceline said.

Vivian winced.

"It *is* cool!" Derrick piped up. "How often do we talk about death and riots? That's awesome! Are we going to have stabbing onstage?"

Okay. Time to change the subject.

"What's that?" Vivian pointed to a blue triangle in the blue water. She only knew it was there because Marceline had used her pen to outline the shape.

"It's a Mako shark," Marceline replied. "Did you know they are the fastest sharks in the world? It also endangers them, which means there aren't a lot of them in the wild."

Huh. Marceline hadn't spoken in a few weeks unless it was reading lines or doing exercises, and then she comes out with this.

"There aren't any sharks in Paris," Vivian said. "It's a great drawing, but I don't see how that makes sense."

She tried to keep her sense of wonder about this. It was bad enough that they were doing *Hunchback*. She didn't want to crush a child's imagination. But they should at least try for some historical accuracy.

Marceline chewed on her braid.

"I like sharks," she said.

"I do too," Vivian admitted. "Sharks are great."

"Why does it matter?" Cosmo asked. "It's just a play."

72

"There's a shark in Harry Potter Land," Derrick said. "I know it's hiding there. Just because it's there doesn't mean that everyone will see it."

Vivian nodded. That was a legitimate point. She knew the shark was there, from a high school graduation trip to Universal Studios.

"I want sharks in our play," Marceline said.

"I want sharks, too," Tara said. "I want to scare the audience!"

She was outnumbered. *Hunchback*, it seemed, would not be historically accurate.

"Okay, why not, then?" Vivian said, thinking about *Big and Bitey in The Loch*. "If we will do this play, let's put in as many sharks as possible in the backdrop. Let the bloodthirsty fish occupy the Seine. Are you sure you want the shark to be blue? I can't see it."

Marceline smiled, showing no teeth. Her fingers moved, and she made the sharks even bluer.

"It's camouflaged," she said. "No one sees sharks in Paris because they match the color of the river."

Yet another remarkable leap of logic that made sense. Vivian made a note to encourage Marceline to take up scriptwriting someday. She'd be a natural at making plot twists happen with plausible explanations.

—

Rehearsals started an hour later. They had to choose their cast. For *Hunchback*, that meant having at least five main characters: Quasimodo, Esmeralda, Frollo, Phoebus, and Clopin. The rest of the cast would have to be the guards, any Romani extras, and Parisian citizens. The King of France would not appear onstage.

"The good news is that we have enough kids for that." Vivian pursed her lips as she reviewed the script. "We can cut out any extra stuff and make sure it doesn't interrupt the flow."

They all sat in the auditorium at the center stage. Vivian handed out copies of scripts. The kids studied the text, which had been typed up and photocopied.

"Are we going to have auditions?" Tara asked.

"We are," Vivian said. "Real actors do auditions. It's also a good way to practice."

"But everyone will get a part," Drew said. "That's one thing that makes it different from a real audition. Most actors and actresses find themselves without a role. We will make sure that you all have a role."

She and Vivian explained the process: several kids would go onstage and read lines with them and the one who read lines best would definitely get the part.

"Who decides who plays who?" Cosmo asked.

"Normally a director would," Vivian said, "but

we don't have one. Drew can be, though. I'll be stage manager, which means I'm in charge of where you stand and where props go."

"I guess I can," Drew said. "I think Xanthia has more experience but she may not have time. Between the two, I'd rather do choreography."

"Dancing?"

"What sort of dancing would you need to do?" Dina asked. She squinted at the stage.

"Probably one with a tambourine." Vivian climbed onto the wooden platform. "It'd be a fast Spanish dance that would grab everyone's attention. This is the dance that makes Frollo entranced with Esmeralda. It has to be magical."

She tapped her sneakers. Sound off one, two, three, four, prepare to stop spinning. Shuffling as the kids moved back to give her room. Drew stayed where she was.

A song played in her head, a tarantallegra spider dance. Then she started spinning on her toes, the way she had in dance class and started to move. Vivian shimmied her shoulders and started clapping up and down. She then moved her toes back and forth. Vivian put her hands on her hips and started running in a circle and backward. Her eyes opened, so she didn't run into anyone.

Energy shot through her. She danced faster, spinning and twirling. Her hands clapped in *presto* speed, and she leaped around the stage. Drew jumped out of the way. Vivian's legs spread, and she finished with a split.

Silence in the auditorium. Vivian took a moment to catch her breath. She hadn't done a dance like that since ballet.

"Something similar to that," she panted.

The kids stared at her.

"That was amazing." Drew recovered her balance. "I didn't know you could dance, girl!"

"You need to be Esmeralda," Cosmo said.

"What?" Vivian and the other girls turned to him. Vivian's dance rhythm faded from her feet.

"I think Cosmo's right," Derrick said. "You're the best dancer. Tara can't do those moves."

"Speak for yourself!" Tara snapped, but her eyes were shining.

"Um." Vivian looked down at her sneakers. "I'm a counselor. The show isn't for me. It's for the rest of you."

"If Tara, Dina, Adaline, and the others are fine with it..." Derrick turned to the girls.

"What does Esmeralda even do?" Adaline asked.

"Depends on the version," Vivian said. "In the Disney version, which we are not doing, she is an activist that defies the crowds. In the original, she falls for a guy that tries to kill her."

"I don't want to be Esmeralda." Adaline wrinkled her nose.

"Me neither," Dina chimed in.

"I do," Tara said. "I can learn that dance. How hard can it be?"

"It's not that hard," Vivian lied. "I can show you the steps, and then you can try them out if you like."

"Why don't you all read the lines, and we can figure out which of you can be Esmeralda," Drew said. "We'll figure it out as we go."

Vivian nodded in relief. She wasn't ready to take charge and insist she wouldn't be doing this part. Tara would make a great Esmeralda.

As if the theater ghosts were laughing at her, a wind blew through. It carried that hot current of rotting flesh. The curtains ruffled, making their rods rattle. Drew shrieked as the wind blew up her skirt, revealing stained underwear.

"Oh not again," Tara said, covering her mouth and nose.

"Ew!" The kids scurried off the stage. Cosmo nearly tripped on the top step, and Adaline pushed Derrick and Dina out of the way. Marcelina simply jumped from the stage to the floor, only grunting as she landed. Tara went down the other set of stairs, the wind rustling her hair.

"Hey, come back," Vivian called. "It's going to go away in a minute."

She was right; the scent faded almost as quickly as it came. The kids stayed offstage though.

"I guess auditions are over." Vivian set down her papers. "Okay, how do we salvage this? Do we do more painting?"

"Sure," Drew said. "Let's get them out of the theater."

Vivian shook her head. She no longer felt the buzz about dancing on stage. For a moment, she had felt like she was at home. Of course, it would help if everyone that was supposed to be here was in the group.

"Marian needs to get an exterminator," she said. "I bet it's dead rats."

"I thought the other counselors had told her ages ago. You know, when some of their kids dropped out."

"I thought so too. But what do I know?" Vivian asked bitterly. "It's not like Marian takes my opinions seriously."

"She better keep the parents happy. Even if they don't get refunds for dropouts."

"Who even dropped out?"

"I don't know." Drew shook her head. "Their names aren't coming to mind."

Vivian groaned. She couldn't remember either. All these random dead meat smells were making her head fog. She wouldn't know if any of her kids had decided to no-show.

They went to the art room and dressed in aprons. Vivian set the younger kids to painting all the sharks that Paris would need for such a fete.

SEVEN

At lunch, the food court was hosting a deal of 50% off cosmetics from the makeup stands. Vivian, in a rare show of sportsmanship, allowed Adaline to try some samples, but warned her that most of these kiosk managers were experts at applying makeup and making it look nice.

"When you get home it's much harder and you realize that they played you for a patsy," Vivian said.

"What's a patsy?" Adaline said.

"A mark. You know, they target you because they think you are easy to fool."

The kiosk manager gave her a dirty glance. She had sparkly blue mascara that made her look like a peacock. It unfortunately didn't improve the wrinkles under her blond bangs.

"You ruin my business, and I will ruin your face," she threatened.

"Bite me," Vivian said. Adaline started giggling. Both women turned to face her.

"Do my face," Adaline ordered through her giggles at Vivian's response. "I'll use my lunch money."

The kiosk manager rolled her eyes. She moved back so Adaline could sit on the polished black stool.

"Now, hold still," the kiosk manager said. "If you want a sample, then you have to prepare for some detailing."

"Okay," Adaline responded. "Just make me look like a star."

The kiosk manager applied eyeshadow and blush. The brush went back and forth with practiced rhythm.

Vivian's legs ached. That complicated dancing routine had nearly done her in. She tried to think of replicating it for Tara, but now the steps wouldn't come to mind. Maybe a theater ghost had possessed her, for that one accidental performance.

Still, her bad mood faded gradually. She waited until Adaline had a layer of sparkly blue eyeshadow and some lip liner. Then Adaline forked over a few dollars and followed Vivian to their usual spot.

The other kids sat at the plastic rectangular tables; Drew included. They had already gotten their food: burgers and fries.

"Here." Drew offered her a shake. "Chocolate swirl. Since you were on makeup duty."

"Thanks." Vivian managed a smile. "That was really nice of you."

It was all so dispiriting. Fewer kids, junk food, and the sense that her job would end in a few months. Of course, her job was ending because she had to go back to college. But she was going to miss moments like this, of camaraderie.

"Something on your mind?" Drew asked.

"Nothing," she replied. A drop of chocolate fell from the plastic cup; she caught it with a napkin. A second later, and it would have stained her shirt with a brown bloom.

"I know you've been working hard." Drew tried to keep her voice down to not interrupt the kid's serious talk about which anime character would be the best at beach volleyball. "And I know you're worried about the changes."

"It's all good," Vivian said. "I'm just tired from the dancing."

That wasn't it. There was a sense of something *wrong* with the theater. Not just the ghosts potentially haunting them or the wind from faulty air conditioning.

"I'm going to run and use the bathroom," Drew said. "Keep an eye on these guys okay?"

"Sure."

"Now we're even." Drew winked as she got up.

"Thanks so much, Vivian." Adaline showed off her makeup to the other kids. "That was so cool to do!"

"Eh, it was nothing," Vivian said. "I can be nice sometimes, you see."

"You've been nice to us *all* the time," Derrick

said.

"Me?" Vivian laughed. "That's not true."

"You've been more patient than the other counselors are," Adaline put in, rubbing at her eyes. "I don't know if Xanthia would ever let me get a makeover."

"Xanthia's nice," Vivian said, a little defensively. "She's been good with the younger kids."

Xanthia, in fact, had handled one of the younger kids wetting themselves, and the kid had cried for hours. She had remained calm, gotten towels and soap, and mopped up the mess all without drawing attention. Drew and Vivian had toasted her at dinner that night and got the egg roll special for her.

Cordy. That had been the kid's name. One of the no-show dropouts. Poor kid; she must have been so embarrassed.

"Well, yes," Derrick said, "but it's not like she or the others listen to us."

Vivian blinked to focus. Cordy's name faded from her mind.

"Point is, something weird is going on in that theater," Adaline said. "I can't say exactly, but it feels like the wind inside is talking to us."

"Talking?" Vivian put down her shake. "What do you mean?"

The kids all looked at each other. A silent signal

seemed to zap between them. Marceline peeled the plastic off her apple pie.

"Terrence wasn't kicked out of camp," Derrick said. "When we had a bathroom break a few weeks ago. He heard that wind calling for him. Then he went down to the basement. We would have followed, but you all called us back. His parents didn't come that day. I guess they forgot about him."

"What?" Vivian said.

"It's true," Cosmo said. "I heard the whole thing. I think someone from the toddler group went down. The girl who peed herself. We haven't seen her since."

Vivian looked at everyone. That name reappeared, again: Cordy. One of Xanthia's kids.

"Is this a joke?" she asked. "Are you all trying to pull my leg?"

"No, ma'am," Dina said. "I've heard it too. And you've probably heard it. Those ghosts?"

She shook her head but was thinking how maybe it did feel like the wind was whispering.

"You see?" Cosmo said. "You've heard it too."

"Why didn't you say anything?" Vivian exclaimed. "Why didn't you tell any of us?"

"Would you have believed us?" Derrick asked. "And it's weird. Every time I think about it, I forget it. Like my brain doesn't want me to remember."

Now that Vivian thought about it, she found it

hard to keep Terrence in mind. His name was like a candle that was flickering on and off, some sort of parlor trick.

"And you're sure they went into the basement?" Vivian asked.

"It calls to us one at a time," Marceline said. "It's calling to me today. I think it's because I painted sharks."

Vivian lost her appetite. She pushed away her milkshake. The chocolate and whipped cream sunk to the bottom of the clear plastic cup.

"Okay, lunch is over," she said, standing.

"What about Drew?" Derrick asked.

"I'll text her." Vivian pulled out her phone.

—

They had attracted more little ones. All of them matching in outer wrappings, if not the same size. Some were tiny and sticklike. Others were larger and burly. It was just like old times.

The portal was getting fuller. Soon they would have to start feasting to make room for the others.

EIGHT

The storeroom looked like someone had tidied with a moth-eaten feather duster. There were spare brooms lying around and a vacuum cleaner with a shredded cord.

"Cool," Derrick said, looking around.

"Not cool," Adaline said. "We're not supposed to be here."

"Just keep your mouth shut and we won't be caught."

"I'm not getting us caught," Adaline said. "It was your idea to tell her. It's going to be your fault."

"No, it won't." Derrick made a sweeping gesture. His fist connected with her arm.

"Ow! VIVIAN!" Adaline shouted. "Derrick hit me."

"Hit him back, and you can call it even," Vivian said, rubbing her eyes. "Aim for the shoulder."

Another punch, and Derrick grunted.

"Now can you knock it off?" Vivian asked with irritation.

Vivian looked at the spare keys of different sizes hanging on a rusty brown hook, next to a mirror that had cracks along the edges. Her own distorted reflection was dusty. Some were bright and shiny silver; she lifted them and took in a new oil smell. Others seemed to be brass and were rusty, like they would unlock a pirate's chest.

She closed her eyes. What would Harper do? He'd use logic and tell her to find the new keys. The basement lock would probably be new, given Marian telling them not to go down. And it would be the one with a lesser amount of dust. She reached for the ring closest to the door which had the newest set of keys. It looked similar to the ones that Harper had borrowed. Had that only been a few weeks ago? A month?

"Everyone, grab a key ring," she said. "I don't want to take chances."

Silence, except the sound of jingling. Then they moved on. Vivian eyed the corridors for more counselors or Marian. All clear so far.

The wind grew stronger as they went down the backstairs. It seemed to call them more. It seemed to be whispering. She ran her fingers against bubbling wallpaper. Once, this had probably been a dignified place to house the building's boiler.

The basement smelled like chicken left to rot in a coffin, even with the door closed. Vivian pressed a hand to her nose. She tried one key. No dice.

"Everyone, stay out here," she said. "Get as far upstairs as you can if I shout. I'm the only one who should get in trouble. And keep a lookout for Marian or the others."

"Okay," Derrick said, nodding to Adaline and Dina. "We'll hold tight to Marceline."

"Good."

She tried another key. It wouldn't even fit. Numbers four and five were also refusing to twist.

Inside, growling noises came. Vivian recoiled and gasped. A few moments, and they faded.

"Did you hear that?" Derrick asked, his voice

low.

"Yes," Marceline squeaked, so softly that it may as well have been the air conditioning.

Vivian took a deep breath. One key to go. She inserted, and twisted. The tumblers within the lock thumped and the door creaked. The kids all leaned back. A curtain of dust fell on Vivian; she wiped it off, coughing. The growls resumed.

"Right," she said. "I'm going in."

"Going in, *towards* that sound?" Adaline asked. "Are you nuts?"

"No," Vivian said. "I'm the adult. And you are the kids. Stay out, all of you."

Still coughing, she walked inside and closed the door behind her to emphasize the point. The hot, rotten breeze hit with force, more putrid than before. Vivian gagged. Roars were getting louder.

I'd rather have a shark right now, she thought. *Sharks don't roar.*

At first, she couldn't see anything. Pitch-black, except for swirls of pink and purple. A zapping sound. That was weird.

She fumbled for the lights. They had to be at the entrance, logically speaking. All lights had to be nearby.

Her hands found the wall. Hot liquid ran over her knuckles. Vivian yelped and moved away. She waved her hand, and wiped it on her jeans. Then she realized it was fake; nothing was attacking and burning her.

"Are you okay?" Derrick called.

"Yeah," Vivian responded, projecting her voice so it went through the door. "I'm fine. Stay up there."

Okay, no switches. Right. Vivian remembered her phone and turned the flashlight app on, hoping she could locate a switch. Piles of cardboard boxes crammed against the wall. Metal shelves held dusty green bowls and manila folders. Some stage props even leaned against the shelves: a shepherd's crook that had the paint peeling off, a wooden leg with a worn kneepad attached, four rusty swords in need of polish, and wads of dirtied cash. It looked fake, at least.

Vivian focused on what was ahead of her. Statues. They were twice her size, with pointy ears and jaws. One had a claw extending. She pointed at them, counting. Five.

"Okay, whoever was in charge of this theater loved monsters," she said. They were occupying most of the hallway in front of her. Almost like guards. Some statues guarded churches...

"Gargoyles," she said aloud. "You're gargoyles. But I never heard of the theater having gargoyles."

She swept her phone light across the basement. Then more purple flashed, blinding her. Her hands fumbled and the phone slipped, spinning the light like a strobe. Its beam bounced a shine off the curved claws.

Vivian blinked, eyes watering. She caught her cellphone and raised it again. The gargoyles had moved. They now had a gap between them, just wide enough for her. She could have sworn...

"VIV!" Derrick again. "You've been down there for a while. All okay?"

"All okay. Stay upstairs!" she called.

Instinct told her to turn around. She should get up, lead the kids out, and tell someone...about creepy statues in a basement? That would get her fired for sure. No, the only way was forward.

"Terrence?" she called. "Cordy? Are you down here?"

Her voice echoed against the walls. Only roars responded. They seemed to be coming from the gargoyles' mouths.

Vivian considered. The gap between the statues was narrow. Still, she could make it, if her legs weren't shaking. She moved, keeping her eyes and cellphone light on them. If she ran out of battery between here and there, she would turn and run.

The stone was rough and flaking in several places. It also felt warm to the touch, like flesh. Vivian was between a wing on one gargoyle and the shoulder of another. If she didn't know any better, she'd think they were waiting for her to get it over with. But that didn't make sense.

"Terrence!" she called. "Come on, kid, don't play

with me! Bang a pipe or something!"

Something rough and warm grabbed the top of her head, lifting her off the ground. Vivian screamed. Another arm went around her waist. Her cellphone fell again, clattering to the ground. The screen cracked, leaving her in semi-darkness.

"They're alive, they're alive!" she screamed, writhing. The gargoyles' mouths opened wider, revealing red tongues that didn't look like stone.

"We're coming!" The door swung open. "Hang on, Viv!"

"NO!" she called. "Stay back!"

Too late; footsteps. Derrick and Marceline were running forward, holding hands. They stopped short, seeing Vivian struggling under the dim cellphone light.

"Run!" she shouted. "Run, you little shits, run!"

Before they could, more gargoyles moved toward them. The two kids looked in askance before backing up, slowly. Vivian knew they weren't going to outrun the statues.

The one holding her, bent down, summoning more light. She shied away from it. A portal appeared, purple and pink, swirling. It looked like the ones from old science-fiction shows. Occasionally, a clawed hand would swipe through it, covered in bristly fur.

Next to the portal, a body slumped, coated in blood and purple light and dressed in tattered jeans.

Eyebrow piercings gleamed under the cellphone beam.

Vivian stared, freezing within the arm holding her. Then she screamed again. It was a raw sound, ragged and hurt, that would make any black-and-white heroine proud of the pain.

"Vivian!" Derrick called, trying to look past the gargoyles.

Her screams died. Purple streaked his skin, and it seemed to have shredded his clothes. She wouldn't have even known if it was him, except for the piercings. Those cursed eyebrow rings dangling beneath the portal light.

"No! No, no, no, *no!* Harper!"

He had discovered it first. He always knew where the keys were.

Vivian retched. Her stomach heaved, but nothing came out. The statue holding her twitched, and it let her go. She crumpled on the ground, falling hard on her ankle.

The portal glowed, winking innocently. Harper lay prone.

Rationally, she ought to have run past the statues to get to the kids. Instinct took over. She ran over, sidestepping the portal. Her hand shook Harper's purple shoulder. The stink shook with him, and she felt cold flesh. Vivian recoiled and screamed again. Dust recoiled throughout the basement from the sound.

"Come on, Harper!" she said. "I need you for this! I need your courage!"

He didn't move. His phone was still in his jeans pocket. It buzzed with phone notifications. All the texts that Drew had sent him. Maybe some from his parents, asking why he didn't call. Maybe they would learn after a bit.

The portal's pink and purple streaks grew stronger. They moved in undulating fingers, like eels underwater. Nothing like sharks, obviously.

Footsteps. Vivian turned, hand over her mouth. There was Marceline, lumbering toward the portal. She had one braid in her mouth and was dragging the other one along the dusty walls. Her eyes were as large as the painted Neptune graffiti they had seen. Derrick was holding onto her, but visibly straining against the effort of keeping her still.

Vivian's thoughts scattered, like the kids on their first day with their questions. She knew that she had to do something. The question was how. Harper had tried something, and he had failed.

Instinct took over; she grabbed Marceline, pulled her away. She was stronger than Derrick and had a grip. Then she faced the portal. Another furry arm swiped through.

"You're not supposed to grab us," Marceline said, her words garbled. Her feet stopped moving. "You could get sued."

Vivian ignored her. She took a step into the

light. This was a bad idea. But it's what Harper would do. It's probably what he tried to do.

More footsteps. Vivian's trance broke when she recognized the tap of those telltale heels.

"Vivian!" Marian called from a haze. "Stop!"

Vivian turned. Her fingertips were brushing the purple light. Electricity tingled through her.

"Stay calm!" Marian shouted. "They won't hurt you if I give the order!"

Realization hit Vivian. That gave her the strength to pull back.

"You knew!" she shouted. "You *knew* he was down here the whole time. And you let us think he was fired!"

"It was an accident," Marian spluttered. "It wasn't me. It was them!"

"Who's 'them?'" Vivian screamed. "These guys, they're your understudies?"

In response, another stone paw swiped through the portal. It vanished. Vivian tried to breathe and found a sob coming out. *Not Harper*. The gargoyles were cornering them. She was going to die here, with the kids.

"So this is what you were doing to keep the theater running?" She could feel the light washing over her. "Taking kids, making people think they had dropped out, and ensuring that those *things* could kill them. What were you *thinking*?"

"I'm restoring the theater to its glory." Marian

waved her hands. "Money won't do it. Neither will talent. I had to make this deal. It begins and ends with me."

"Harper never did a no-show." Tears pricked Vivian's eyes. "He found out what you were doing. And he tried to stop you. Or *them*, whatever 'them' are."

She could picture it; Harper's eyebrows going up with the piercings, the sound of his yells echoing through the basement. His body slumping after the portal zapped him.

"He never understood." Marian's face betrayed anguish. "I never wanted this. It was just going to be a few kids and trespassers, and everything would open up again, the way it's supposed to be."

Vivian shook her head. She could feel hands tugging her back, wanting her to enter. They were beckoning, wanting her to step through and join the kids.

"You can't have a theater without people," she said. "And especially if you are killing them.'

Maybe she didn't need to put her whole body in; she just needed to offer a hand. And she did, thrusting her arm into the portal.

"Stop that!" Marian stumbled on her heels. "You'll only get yourself killed!"

Pain ran through Vivian's arm as if she was burning on Eris' lamp. More screaming and it tore her throat apart from the effort. She reached, found hands reaching for her. Then she pulled back. It was time to be a shark and to latch on to the nearest body part she couldn't see. A glimpse of hair. Terrence's curls. He was *alive*. Then that meant...

"Hold tight!" she shouted.

Thank goodness for all the exercise from dancing, and her doing some weight lifting with the props and boxes. She ground her sneakers and kept pulling back, whatever it was.

Marian ran forward. Her eyes gleamed with sad malice. Vivian was trapped by whatever would pull her in or refused to come out.

Derrick trained his eyes on the sprinting woman and leaned out his foot. Marian tripped over his shoe and stumbled. A snap and her heel broke.

"Oof," Miriam said arms pin-wheeling for balance.

Vivian let go of the thing she'd grabbed and looked over her shoulder just in time. She sidestepped Marian, who sailed into the portal.

A boom and a flash of light. A body tossed in the air. Screaming. Vivian wasn't sure if it was her. Everything was chaos. Dust and fetid and sticky blood rained about the dim room.

The gargoyles roared in her face and thrashed. They sounded like lions with mouths full of dust. They beat their wings, and spread more of the blood.

Then the light faded. Vivian rubbed her face to make sure she could see. She blinked.

The gargoyles had vanished. So had Marian. The others slumped on the floor. Terrence and Derrick huddled close to each other. Marceline leaned against the wall, hands wrapped around a little girl who could only be Cordy. Vivian curled next to Harper's body.

"It smells like something died in here." Terrence rubbed his eyes. Blood dripped from his ears and nose. It started to stain his shirt.

Vivian scooted away from Harper. She brought her knees to her chest. Her breaths came in, and then out, rapidly. She was hyperventilating.

"What happened?" Derrick asked. He checked a bump on Terrence's forehead.

"Marian was the one who made the deal," Vivian panted. "Once Marian was gone, the deal was off. Simple villain death."

The kids stared at her blankly. Marceline opened her mouth. The wet braid fell against her shirt. She looked astonished, an expression that removed years from her frame. Derrick rubbed his eyes.

"I take it back," he said. "I never want to come down here again."

"Me neither," Vivian agreed. "Everyone okay? Anyone missing?"

"Marian is," Marceline said.

"No statues," Derrick said.

"Right." Vivian took a deep breath. This was all so hard to take in: Marian made a deal with theater demons. That these demons existed in the first place and cared about the art. Also, that Harper was decomposing next to her.

"Oh my God," Terrence said. "I swear, I didn't mean to come down here. One moment I was upstairs, next—"

"We believe you." Derrick patted him with some sympathy.

"Who's got service?" Vivian asked. "We need to call nine-one-one."

Marceline crawled onto the floor. She reached for Vivian's cellphone before handing it to her.

NINE

She walked and talked in a daze, letting the police give her a blanket and coffee. Vivian wrapped herself in it, letting the standard wool envelop her. Her answers garbled out of her like swirling spaghetti, trying to explain what was down there.

"That damn theater," the cop interviewing her said. He typed notes on his tablet. "I was working there on the *Annie* case. Remember those girls?"

Vivian nodded. That memory seemed to come from a faint distance, like a dream. Yes. Those five girls.

"Same story, except this time we have a body."

She couldn't even register his words. But Vivian managed a shrug.

"You got that right," she croaked. "Do I have to stay here for longer?"

"We've called someone to pick you up." The cop patted her on the shoulder. "Your emergency contact."

Vivian stared at the coffee swirling in the cup they had given her. There hadn't been a body for Marian. Was she going to get a funeral? Did she deserve one?

"Hey."

Vivian looked up. It was Eris, dressed in pajamas and a t-shirt that had a giant fermata on it. Eris had never looked so wild, with her hair out of place. She must have been sleeping from sunset to sunrise, the way she did to make up for all-nighters.

"You're my emergency contact?" Vivian asked. She couldn't even think of her contact list.

"Yeah. They called from your cellphone when you entered a state of shock. Not that I blame you. But it was either me or your mother and your mom can't get down here yet."

Vivian felt her shoulders relax. This blanket was chafing rather than comforting her and her coffee was not right for having that late in the evening.

"You okay?" Eris asked.

Vivian shrugged. She actually wasn't. There was the smell of rotting chicken, and she wondered if dead bodies could turn a person vegetarian.

"Come on, then. I'm going to cram you full of candy and shark movies. Or romantic comedies. Maybe we should avoid the blood and gore for now?"

"Maybe," Vivian said. "All the blood in the movies is corn syrup though. You can tell it's not real."

"Okay." Eris nodded. "We're taking you to my place."

Vivian removed her blanket. She folded it and returned it to the police officer who had given it to her. He nodded, with some gruffness and sympathy.

"Thanks for saving those kids," he said. "You're a hero."

Hero. Ha. She didn't feel like one any more than she felt like the nice counselor.

Eris fortunately had a car, or this would be so much harder. She had parked in the lot, an old Camry that had seen better days with the back windows stuck. No theater-parking permit on her dashboard window.

"Did the security guard give you trouble?"

Vivian asked. "They make all the campers pay for parking."

"I'm not paying them shit," Eris said. "Not after what happened."

No guards, Vivian realized, looking around. No one had stayed after they had gotten wind of a dead body.

She opened the passenger side and helped Vivian in, even buckling her seatbelt. Vivian realized she was still holding her terrible bitter coffee and glugged it in one go. Then she placed it in the cup-holder.

"We thought he was fired," she said, as Eris put the key in the ignition. "That's what Marian let us think. And it seemed to make sense. How can he be gone? How could she have *left* him like that?"

"She knew? Seriously?"

"She knew." The details spilled out of Vivian, with more clarity than they had before.

"My God," Eris said. "I'm so sorry. He was your friend?"

Vivian nodded. Part of her was still in that basement, screaming at the sight of Harper's body. He had been so alive.

"I guess we know why it was a haunted theater," she sighed. "Man, we are all totally going to lose our jobs."

"It wasn't your fault. You didn't know that the camp administrator was doing a ritual sacrifices."

"We should have known."

"Well, from what I heard you did do something." Eris turned right onto the road. "Something amazing."

"It doesn't feel amazing."

"It never does when someone dies."

Vivian leaned against the car window. She dared not let her eyes close. Harper's smell would rise with the wind that ghosts would send through the theater to warn of wrongdoing. Perhaps that's what they were doing.

The ride was slow, because Eris was going against traffic. Outside, drivers yelled at each other through deafening levels of rock music or NPR or podcasts. Eris rolled up the windows and put on some classical music.

"You know what's funny?" she said. "We were watching shark movies when you found out that you got the job. You were so excited."

Vivian smiled wanly. She remembered that day. Only about a month ago, but it may have been in another lifetime. Maybe it had happened to someone else.

"That shark movie must have been some sort of luck. You got the job. And the next time we did sharks, you got to chill from your rough first day."

"I thought it was good luck, but I was worried about Harper," Vivian said. "Oh my god, he is dead. Harper was dead for a month, Eris. And we didn't know."

"It's okay." Eris' trimmed fingernails on her shoulder, patting it. "It's okay."

Something tapped the car roof. It seemed to be experimentally touching something.

"What the hell?" Eris ducked instinctively and swerved to the curb and put the shifter in park. "Are we getting hail?"

Vivian shook her head. She reached to the ceiling and traced the dent that had appeared.

"'A claw," she said, thinking and then her eyes grew wide. "Like the one that grabbed me."

"Oh for fuck's sake." Eris grabbed the shifter and wheel and pressed her foot to the pedal. "Thank you for no traffic."

She zoomed forward, and Vivian heard a whooshing around. She whirled her head as something large fell to the road and shattered. Dust filled the air, along with honking cars and screeching tires. The crashes were deafening; she covered her ears.

This wasn't over. Damn.

TEN

Being on the train again helped Vivian adjust. She hadn't worn a suit since her job interview. That had felt like a lifetime ago. This time, Eris had let her borrow an outfit. It wasn't funeral clothes, but it would do.

At night, you could see the sunset through the train windows. There were fewer people who took the 7:00 PM one, so Vivian could take a window seat. She looked at the sun going behind the buildings and into the bay. The roof had a better view, but Vivian doubted that they would be allowed to go on the roof at all today.

It was easier today. She had found Harper's dead body and a portal to another world only about seventy hours before. If the superintendent hadn't texted that he had finally fixed that stupid faucet, she wouldn't have gotten the strength to drag herself off Eris' couch, or the willpower to get three concerned cats off her chest. But she had managed to read another text—an invitation. So she had asked Eris for a change of clothes. And maybe some toothpaste.

Eris asked her she thought it was safe. They'd made a mad dash from the car after the incident with the gargoyle, but there'd been no trace of the creatures since.

"Maybe it wasn't what I thought," Vivian said. "Likely just lingering paranoia, and a big bird."

Eris shook her head gently but did not argue. She had stayed with her that night, and they found videos to watch on the laptop.

Harper's favorite takeout place had a dinner menu. She found the group outside, all dressed in black or blue. They had taken a table that overlooked the street, where people walked their dogs.

"Hey there." Drew sipped water. She looked so much skinnier. "I got you a bubble milk tea."

"Thanks." Vivian took it and started sipping. Not coffee this time. Just milk and some black Boba to chew on with her thoughts.

"I'm glad you came," Xanthia said. "To be honest, it still feels unreal."

"I keep expecting him to show up," Vivian said. "And steal all of our egg rolls and give us fortune cookies."

"It's my fault," Drew said. "I should have realized something was wrong when he didn't read his texts for months. Who does that?"

"No, it was me," Xanthia said. "I should have stopped him. If I hadn't been going along with his crazy plans to explore every part of the theater."

"It wasn't anyone's fault," Vivian said. "Except Marian's. She got him killed."

They all sat. Vivian swirled the straw in her tea. She slurped some more Boba into her mouth and chewed.

"His parents are going to host a memorial," Drew said. "They're flying down here for it and then burying him up in Georgia. We should go and raise hell."

"Why?" Sallie asked.

"They're going to take out all his piercings."

Vivian tried not to choke on her tapioca bubbles. A laugh nearly sputtered out with a mouthful of milk tea.

"Harper would hate that," Xanthia smirked through doleful eyes. "He would be so mad and rise back from the dead to make them put the eyebrow rings back in. You know he would."

Giggles echoed around the table. For the first time, some weight lifted off Vivian's chest.

"I remember how he made Marian angry so she wouldn't focus on me being late," Vivian said. "He was always really nice to me and made sure that I felt welcome."

"He did the same for me," Sallie said from the end of the table. "I was so shy and nervous, and he told me not to be scared of the kids. They're little monsters, he said, but they're still people."

"So it seems that Derrick's mother is taking over," Drew said. "She's going to get the camp run as is. So, we can get our paycheck."

"Why?" Xanthia burst out. "Someone died. Harper died! That camp should be closed!"

"Beats me." Drew said. "This is just what I heard. Means we may not be out of a job yet."

"I'm not going back," Sallie said. "I can't step foot in that theater again."

"By the way, I ordered something already." Drew looked around. "Be prepared."

"For what?" Vivian asked.

Their server brought a giant plateful of egg rolls. There were twenty, and about four different kinds of sauces. All the counselors stared at each other. Steam wafted off the rolls, along with glistening layers of sesame oil. The grease awakened Vivian's appetite.

"It felt like the best way to honor him," Xanthia shrugged. "We all get a student discount anyway."

They all watched the plate. No one wanted to be the first one to take a bite. Vivian knew that Sallie was vegetarian and didn't want to bite into pork and wonton paper. Not that she blamed Sallie. Anything meat-related made her feel so queasy these days.

"To Harper, the best leader we could have." Vivian grabbed a roll and lifted it. Harper would've chided her for wasting takeout.

"Yes, to Harper." Xanthia followed her lead and lifted one roll. "Someone who made us feel safe and welcome, in a theater that was neither of those things."

"Cheers!" They all held their rolls toward each other. Flakes of wonton crumbled down and coated the table. Half a roll fell off and splashed into Drew's water glass.

Something else fell out of the fried wonton

wrapping. It was grey and crackly, and sunk to the bottom of the glass. Drew stared at it.

"What is that?"

Vivian broke open her roll. It had a stone claw in it, small but carved into a sharp triangle. She looked at it, and her appetite vanished.

"Um, can we get the check?" Xanthia asked. Her face had gone green, as she had bitten one of the claws. She spat it out, and it lay on her plate, gleaming.

"What's going on here?" Vivian asked. "They're gone. They have to be."

—

Back to the ice cream night shift over the weekends. Now it was her only job, at least until the people that owned the theater decided if they could open up the camp and avoid the liability. Vivian had been paid for the weeks she had put into the camp as a counselor, but after that, their future was in limbo. She would need another job, and despite what Sallie had said, she could still go back and stand on the stage. The gargoyles were no longer there; they couldn't be. The counselors would all have to wait for a miracle, or for the board to officially shut down the Haunted Basilio Theater camp.

"You okay, Vivian?" her boss asked. "You look tired."

"I'm fine." She forced a smile. "Don't think you're getting rid of me that easily. Unlike the teens you hired to replace me, I don't have a curfew."

"That's the spirit." He clapped her back. If she didn't know that he had a husband, she would have taken that differently. "Why don't you get yourself a scoop of gelato and then park yourself behind the front counter? We seem to have some Nutella."

For the first time ever, she shot him a grateful look. It's not like the entire story had gotten out, with her testing the locks in the basement, but perhaps he had sensed that she needed a scoop.

Her apron went on, and she helped herself to some Nutella gelato in a plastic bowl. The cool taste made her think. There was still no explanation for the way that things had gone down. At least, there was nothing that had made sense in any tangible fashion.

The newspaper had managed to get a story on what had happened; some nut had claimed that the theater had been founded as part of a deal with the devil. The theater needed to swallow a child once in a few years, or the owners would never be happy. Marian's body hadn't been found, and the kids who had been taken couldn't exactly explain what happened.

A few years ago, Vivian would have laughed it off as something an illegal tour guide would announce to make sure that his audience would sneak inside. Now instead she had chills at the thought of any devil that liked pink and purple. She would much prefer to get brain freeze from swallowing her gelato too fast to make it on time to her shift.

She served all the kids who came with their parents to watch a movie. They all looked so free and unburdened. None of them had heard the siren call of a stage theater that had a new padlock over the oldest room, one that would swallow you alive and leave corpses of adults to rot on the floor. These kids had never seen a dead body, except for on the screen.

The plastic cup went in the garbage. Vivian wiped her mouth with a napkin and tossed that as well. The sound was very satisfying.

"Vivian." A woman in a white coat and dark brown loafers stood. "There you are."

"Hello," Vivian said, putting on her most professional smile. "Do I know you?"

"No," the woman admitted. "We never met."

"What can I get you?"

"I wanted to thank you."

"Huh?" Vivian blinked. She was a zombie on this shift, but she wasn't sure that her hearing had completely gone like that. "Sorry? I didn't serve you yet."

"Oh. I'm sorry." The woman looked sheepish. "That Nutella looks good. I'll have that."

"Coming right up." Vivian replaced her smile and got a new cup. "Now you can thank me."

"I'm Derrick's mother. He told me what you did."

Vivian dropped the scoop. It fell into the vanilla tub. She didn't retrieve it. The cup crumpled in her hands.

"Um," she said.

"Thank you," Derrick's mother said. "You saved him."

Then, in a manner that didn't seem to fit her small-but-slim frame, she reached over and wrapped an arm around Vivian's shoulders in a half-hug. If the counter had separated them and Vivian's apron weren't covered in vanilla ice cream splatters. She knew that she didn't want to make that nice white coat sticky.

"I didn't do anything, ma'am," she said. "All I did was listen to the kids."

"And you did listen to them at the right time." Derrick's mother released her. "No one else did."

But the kids hadn't told anyone else. Maybe that was what had made it right. Perhaps Vivian by taking some time to talk to them and treating them like adults had opened the floodgates and told her to go into that basement.

Derrick's mother pressed her lips together. "You stopped it before Derrick was lured down there. Thank you, again."

"I guess you're here to tell me that I can be a camp counselor again?" Vivian asked.

"Actually, yes. I would have texted you, but I wanted to give my thanks in person. It's listed on your resume that you worked here."

That cursed resume. Still, Vivian stared.

"Are you serious? It could reopen?"

"You could teach the kids again, and I plan to officially reopen the camp next year," Derrick's mother said. "This would just be a small group, as a means of putting on the shows the kids were planning."

"I don't get it. I thought the theater was dead."

"Derrick is sad that he can't act in the play," Derrick's mother said. "And I am sad that a lot of these kids won't be able to enjoy the theater experience after what happened. Quite a few are going into sports camps, so only about three or four are still interested. The ones that want to come back, want to see what putting on a show is like."

That sounded nice. Because the first rule of the stage was that the show had to go on, even with dire circumstances of people being eaten.

"We want to bring back most of the crew," she said. "To show that we aren't like Marian. Not all of us administrators care about the money and numbers. We have children, you know."

That made sense, in a twisted way. Prove there were no curse and no temptations that could hurt someone. Then they could perform and sing and find a way to fight back the demons.

"But why do you want us back, ma'am?"

"You've all been good counselors. I've seen your evaluation reports."

"Have you approached anyone else?" Vivian asked. She didn't hide her sardonic tone. Everyone else was probably trying to find a last-minute job in the interim, except for Sallie. That girl hadn't even *been* in the basement, but she seemed to have lost her taste for theater. It was a shame since her carpools had been great.

"You'd be the first. I want to gauge interest since you were the one at the center of all this."

Vivian considered. Was she the center? If everything was pushed into the light and out of the basement, did that mean it went somewhere else?

"You're such a big part of the theater."

Vivian looked past the woman. Something swooped just outside the ice-cream parlor. Stone eyes met her gaze.

Marian said she didn't want to kill anyone, Vivian thought. *But all it takes is one desperate person making a deal. Like Derrick's mother.*

"What if I don't want to?" Vivian said, still eyeing the world beyond the ice cream shop.

Derrick's mother leaned over the counter and whispered, "You're the center of this, I don't think you have a choice."

ELEVEN

Opening Night:

The stage lights made all the kids sweat. They trundled on and off the stage repeating their lines. This play was simple, about a teacher trying to educate a bunch of kids for whom she substituted. So many puns.

Vivian ran through the lines in her head: "I am Esmeralda, Romani, and woman of Paris. They say I am just a girl, but I know so much about the world."

She wiped some sweat off her bangles. It would not do to make a fool of herself in front of these people, on the stage that she had once coveted as a child. She had asked for skin-colored moccasins. She kicked at them with ease.

Things had changed little since the kids had exited the portal. Yes, her kids had been behaving better and also acting wildly at the same time. Their frenetic fear had faded though they had taken much delight in the "stage left, stage right" game that taught them about which places defined which on the stage. They enjoyed sitting with her at the food court and were less likely to run off. Marceline still kept asking about the roof, though. She had painted many sharks into the Paris backdrop, and had even sneaked a whale shark into the Seine.

It was their parents that had changed, in all honesty. Derrick's mother—Vivian had to remember to call her Bernadette—made all the difference as a parent running the show. With Marian out of the picture, a wealthy hedge fund manager like Derrick's mother could afford to buy the shares and convince people to listen to her while looking the other direction about how fast her takeover had been.

Derrick's mother promised that one day the Basilio Theater would run for real, with proper performances. There would be no curse, no one sacrificed. Part of the reason Vivian kept working was to make sure that Bernadette lived up to that promise. One day Derrick would grow up, and people would forget what children were like.

A few parents came just to pick up the kids before, and they came and talked to Vivian, thanking her for what she had done. One turned out to run a theater in the nearby city and invited her for auditions in the fall. Another said that Vivian could take a job with them at their company as a clerk. It would pay more than being a counselor. She would think about it, because she wasn't the secretary type—and if she was honest, could she really leave the Basilio?

Vivian adjusted her wig. Esmeralda in this version had poufy black hair. She had to ensure that none of her bangles or necklaces fell off from all the dancing. The dress needed some layers of velvet to hide the moth-eaten parts, but the tailor they had hired last minutes had done a great job. Some days you just needed a taste of perfection to forget walking into a portal.

Dress rehearsal had gone well, even if the director was a traumatized fellow counselor. Xanthia had been providing stage directions and helping the kids with their lines. She had dark circles under her eyes and jumped at every shadow.

Acting in rehearsals made Vivian forget seeing Harper's body in the void. She'd probably need therapy once she went back to school in the fall. Eris had been providing all the shark movies and beer as a temporary remedy. She hadn't asked about it.

No need to think about that now. There was a show to perform, a job to do. She could break down later after the cast party with the kids. Terrence had designed quite a cool way to introduce the Parisian dawns and mist with dry ice. He had also done quite a choreography number.

Tara was already marching around onstage, dressed as Clopin. She had insisted on doing her own makeup for this one and had wanted to add a star to her nose. It didn't fit the jester look, but Vivian would not quibble. It beat arguing with Tara over lunch about who the best superhero was.

"Now are you ready to get on all fours?" Vivian asked.

In response, Derrick crouched. He gave a little "baa."

"Not too early," Vivian whispered, trying not to laugh. Though a goat braying off-screen would work for this version of the story where 19th century Paris was chaotic and fun. No French Revolution with beheading, no teenage queens that were framed for crimes of hedonism.

She took a deep breath and thought of her character. Naive Esmeralda, trying to make a living in a world that would soon either kill or break her. They had cut the part about Phoebus successfully hanging Esmeralda, so that the parents wouldn't riot against an obvious tragedy. Instead, she would spend her life in Notre Dame, away from everyone else but with Quasimodo as her platonic companion. It would be a bittersweet ending, but it would be fair. Fair to the kids, who probably had seen more than their fair share of death.

Vivian took a deep breath. The character settled around her: a naive girl ready to tackle the city of Paris. Her lines rang in her head. She would be a teenager, with no worry, for a couple of hours.

The curtains drew back and a breeze that had followed her like a blackfly since her return fell upon her, invading the folds of her dress and then the pores of her skin. It had a semi-rotten smell, that reminded her of the basement.

Vivian paused mid-breath. She tried not to gasp; it would mess with her mic. The gargoyles in there hadn't disappeared, but only resettled to lay dormant until the right moment arose. This time she didn't have any keys.

It was showtime, and she had to make her entrance. Her left foot shot out as if of its own accord, and she danced.

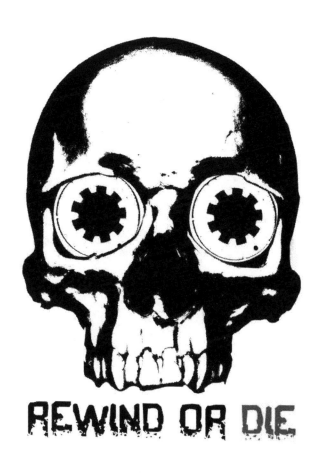

REWIND OR DIE

REWIND OR DIE

Midnight Exhibit Vol. 1
Infested - Carol Gore
Benny Rose: The Cannibal King - Hailey Piper - Jan. 23
Cirque Berserk - Jessica Guess - Feb. 20
Hairspray and Switchblades - V. Castro - Feb. 20
Sole Survivor - Zachary Ashford - Mar. 26
Food Fright - Nico Bell - Mar. 26
Hell's Bells - Lisa Quigley - May 28
The Kelping - Jan Stinchcomb - May 28
Trampled Crown - Kirby Kellogg - Jun. 25
Dead and Breakfast - Gary Buller - Jun. 25
Blood Lake Monster - Renee Miller - Jul. 23
The Catcreeper - Kevin Lewis - Jul. 23
All You Need is Love and a Strong Electric Current -
Mackenzie Kiera - Aug. 27
Tales From the Meat Wagon - Eddie Generous - Aug. 27
Hooker - M. Lopes da Silva - Oct. 29
Offstage Offerings - Priya Sridhar - Oct. 29
Dead Eyes - EV Knight - Nov. 26
Dancing on the Edge of a Blade - Todd Rigney - Dec. 12
Midnight Exhibit Vol. 2 - Dec. 12

www.UNNERVINGMAGAZINE.com